The Cloud Chronicles: Annunciation

E.S. Fortune
&
Emily Regan

ISBN: 978-0-9987732-2-3

Cover design by Katie McLeod

First Edition

The Cloud Chronicles: Annunciation

E.S. Fortune

&

Emily Regan

Chapter 1

As Kate Porter jogged along the New York city streets, the shrill bleat of her cell phone broke the rhythmic, meditative metronome of her feet on the pavement. She looked at the screen and sighed.

"Hello?" Kate asked breathlessly as she answered the call, bending over to rest a hand on her sweaty knee. It slipped, but she caught her balance.

"Where are you?"

"Hello to you too, Claire," Kate said, rolling her eyes.

"Do you know what's happening today?" Claire asked impatiently.

"Of course I do, we've all known about it for the last two weeks."

"It's been getting lower, it's actually going to land today."

"I know, Claire," Kate said, glancing down the street. Central Park wasn't far away and the spaceship was still hovering overhead, looming ominously. Even from where she stood, Kate could see the extensive blockades, armed guards, and tanks. "I'm looking at it right now."

"You'd better get back here soon, we cannot be late today."

"I know, I know. I'm heading back now."

Kate said goodbye and hung up the phone before turning and jogging back in the direction of her apartment building.

Kate breathed hard as she rounded the last corner. Up ahead, she saw her apartment building and she knew she was so close to finishing, which made this block that much harder. The stitch in her side threatened to split but she forced herself to keep jogging. *One, two, three, one, two, three* Kate silently counted in her head with each footfall on the pavement, trying to keep herself from focusing on her lungs burning in her chest. She usually jogged in Central Park but since it was blocked off, she'd had to improvise around her neighborhood and had grossly overestimated her endurance. Finally, she slowed as she reached the building's entrance--and promptly tripped on a large crack in the sidewalk. Kate landed hard on her hands and knees and felt pain flare across her left hand. She stood up slowly and looked at her palms. A sharp point on the sidewalk had cut her left hand, a rough line across her skin, and blood slowly welled over the wound. Kate brushed her uninjured hand on her running shorts and sighed. The cut didn't hurt all that much; mostly, she just felt disgusted at the thought of touching a New York City sidewalk with her bare hands, let alone giving the filth an entry point into her body. Plus, since today was the big day, Kate didn't take tripping as a good omen. With her luck, she'd end up with some sort of super bacterial infection that was resistant to antibiotics and her hand would fall off while the rest of the world got to witness the first human interaction with extraterrestrials in history.

Kate walked through the front door of her building and made her way up the six flights of narrow stairs that led to her apartment. The second landing smelled vaguely of urine and Kate's nose wrinkled involuntarily at the smell. But, in all fairness, she supposed urine was a better option than its counterpart. Kate couldn't imagine that she smelled great after her run, but at least she didn't smell like an outhouse. At least, she hoped she didn't. She had no idea if Claire had already showered or not, but Kate knew that if the shower was open, she'd have to take it immediately or risk going to work covered in jogger sweat. She unlocked the door quietly and snuck inside, slipping off her running shoes as quickly and as silently as she could. She picked them up and listened for the shower--nothing. There was barely any noise in the apartment at all. Kate wondered where Claire was; she knew from the phone call that Claire hadn't slept through her alarm. Kate smiled to herself at the thought of Claire ever sleeping in. In the years she'd known her, Kate had never seen Claire do anything as abhorrent to her type A sensibilities as sleeping late. Kate, on the other hand, loved to sleep in. Not that she'd gotten to do much of it since she and Claire became roommates in college. However, when she stayed the occasional night at her mother's house, there was nothing more delicious to Kate than forgoing an alarm clock and allowing herself to be awoken by the late morning sun when he finally tried to break through the blinds, cocooned in soft, warm blankets. Although she generally liked sharing an apartment with Claire, Kate was somewhat looking forward to the day when she'd be able to afford her own apartment. Granted, anything she'd be able to afford in the foreseeable future was not likely to be bigger than a breadbox, but the idea of having her own breadbox was intoxicating.

Kate turned towards the tiny bathroom just as Claire opened the door to the small bedroom they shared, split down the middle with a folding screen. They locked eyes for a moment before they both broke into a sprint for the bathroom. Kate got there first and leaped inside, slamming the door behind her and clicking the push lock that was only somewhat reliable. Claire kicked the door, her foot causing a loud thump to reverberate in the small bathroom. The lock barely held, although one more swift kick to the door might have been its undoing.

"God dammit, Kate! I really need to shower before work!" she yelled through the door as Kate turned on the shower.

"So do I!" Kate called back as she stripped off her clothes and dropped them into a pile on the floor. She stuck her left hand under the meager shower stream to rinse off the blood, and was pleased to note that the water had risen in temperature from freezing to tepid. "I just got back from running and I'm all sweaty. I have to shower."

"I'm not responsible for your stupid fitness choices!" Claire called through the door. Kate could hear the frustration fading from Claire's voice and she smiled.

"I'll be quick, I promise," Kate said as she pulled back the shower curtain and stepped under the water that, optimistically, could possibly be referred to as warm.

"You know, this would be a lot easier if you'd just let me in the bathroom so I could brush my teeth or something," Claire said. "I've known you since freshman year, you don't have to be weird about sharing a bathroom just because you're naked."

"Sorry, can't hear you!" Kate called back as she squirted a large dollop of shampoo into her uninjured hand and began to massage it into her hair.

"Sure you can't," Claire called sarcastically. Kate could imagine Claire rolling her eyes. It was a sight with which Kate was quite familiar. "Just hurry up."

"No comprendo!" Kate yelled back as she stuck her head under the water. She kept meaning to talk to the landlord about the water pressure but it kept slipping her mind. Claire actually liked the weak pressure, she said she liked the eco-consciousness of it. Kate, on the other hand, was willing to sacrifice a few fishes if it meant she could take a decent shower with more than just the suggestion of water.

Kate bathed as quickly as she could and shut off the shower, hoping there would be at least a little warm water left for Claire. It occurred to her as she toweled off that she'd never had to fight for the bathroom with their other roommate, Kim. In fact, Kate wasn't sure she'd ever seen Kim take a shower since she moved in two months ago. The city was currently experiencing a heat wave and with parts of the city smelling like hot garbage, Kate didn't know how Kim was getting by without bathing. Kate knew that Kim probably just bathed while she and Claire were asleep or at work, but all the same, Kate still found it weird. Not that she even saw Kim all that often. Kim had a room to herself but it was almost laughable to refer to it as a bedroom since it was barely bigger than a linen closet. A rat would've found Kim's room cramped. But Kim didn't seem to mind or, at least, Kate didn't think she did. It's difficult to judge someone's level of comfort when you almost never see them.

The cut on her hand was still active so Kate checked under the sink for the battered first aid kit she'd found under there when she and Claire had first moved in. She was disappointed to find it mostly empty aside from a handful of tiny circular plasters that looked barely big enough to cover a pimple, let alone a scrape across her palm, and an loosely rolled elastic bandage. Kate grabbed a wad of tissue paper and pressed it against her hand before wrapping it in place with the bandage. She figured she could check the first aid kit at the office for something more substantial later. Kate wrapped her towel around her body and opened the bathroom door to find Claire standing directly outside, her arms impatiently crossed over her chest.

"Did you wait here the whole time?" Kate asked. Claire said nothing and pushed past her into the humid bathroom and shut the door behind her, leaving Kate standing by herself in the narrow hallway. That, Kate supposed, answered that. Kate shrugged her shoulders and padded down the hallway lined with thin, threadbare carpet to their bedroom. She dressed and reopened the bedroom door, glancing over at the bathroom door, still shut tight. She knew she was unlikely to get a crack at the hairdryer before it was time to leave, so she just toweled off her hair and ran her fingers through it as best she could.

Thirty minutes later, Claire was standing at the door, impatiently tapping her foot while Kate shoved a piece of toast in her mouth. Kate noted how severe Claire looked, her blonde hair pulled back into a tight bun, the fitted black pantsuit, the high heels. Kate thought Claire looked like she was about to start a board meeting for a multinational corporation or like a restaurant patron who was about to insist on speaking to a manager. Either way, Kate felt like a hot mess next to her with loose brown hair and bandaged hand.

"Okay, let's go," Kate said around the bread, her words a little muffled. Claire looked slightly disgusted as Kate talked with her mouth full.

"What did you do to your hand?" Claire asked, noticing the bandage for the first time as they exited the apartment. Claire pulled out a neat key ring and locked the front door. Kate's own keys, lost somewhere in the abyss of her purse, were on a cluttered, scratched key ring that had long ago lost its charm. Kate wasn't even sure what half of the keys belonged to, but she was afraid to throw any of them away and so instead she just kept adding and adding.

"Tripped on the sidewalk this morning," Kate mumbled through a mouthful of toast.

"You know you're probably going to end up with some kind of super bacterial infection that's resistant to antibiotics, right?"

Kate nodded and the two friends walked down the stairs together, Kate once again marveling at how Claire seemed to effortlessly navigate the stairs in heels while Kate wished she were wearing her running shoes instead of her work flats. They left the building and headed down the street together to the subway station before descending into the bowels of New York City. Kate smiled at the guy playing classic 60s rock covers, wishing she had some cash to toss in his guitar case, and stood with Claire on the platform.

"So, today's the day," Claire said, smiling nervously. Kate could hear that the other commuters were having similar conversations as the train pulled in.

"Yup. I think my uncle said it's supposed to land sometime tonight."

"In Central Park, right?" Claire asked as they boarded the subway train together. Kate nodded. "What do you think they want?"

Kate shrugged.

"I don't know. I'd assume they're peaceful though. I mean, if they wanted to blow us up I think they would've done it by now," she said.

"True," Claire agreed.

A few stops later, Kate and Claire disembarked and headed up to the surface, breaking into the morning air, and walked the four blocks to the offices of the New York Eye. It was one of the city's least popular newspapers, but it was the only place that had been willing to hire two recent college graduates who didn't have the three to five years of experience required for most entry level jobs at the bigger, more prominent newspapers. The reception area wasn't exactly modern or inviting and it desperately needed a fresh coat of paint, but it was clean. Kate wasn't sure if the fake ficus in the corner actually brightened the room as intended or made the room slightly more depressing, but she chose not to think about it too much. The newsroom was a little better, and Kate was honestly just happy to have her own desk. The editor-in-chief, Barry, was nice enough, if perpetually exhausted, and all around, it was an okay job. Kate hoped one day to work for somewhere more prominent, but this was fine for now. At the very least, it was a legitimate newspaper to put on her resume.

Around noon, Claire stopped by Kate's desk.

"Oh, hey, do you want to go get lunch?" Kate asked.

"I have a better idea," Claire said, sitting on the edge of the desk. "Actually, it's a brilliant idea."

"Oh?"

"I can't believe I didn't think of it sooner," Claire said. "You," she started, pausing for dramatic effect, "should call your uncle."

"I'm pretty sure he's busy today," Kate said. "You know, spaceship? Aliens?"

Claire rolled her eyes.

"That's the point! He can get you in!"

"What do you mean 'in'?" Kate asked, not liking the direction of this conversation.

"Look," Claire said. "he's going to be there, right?"

"Yeah . . ." Kate said slowly.

"So he could take you with him! You could get press access that no one else can. The Eye could get the most exclusive story in human history! Do you know what that would do for the paper? Not to mention your career."

Kate considered this.

"I don't know . . . it's not that I don't want to, I've just been trying to give my uncle some space while all this is happening. Space--ha," Kate said, chuckling at her own unintentional joke. Claire didn't laugh.

"Well, I already talked to Barry and he thinks it's a great idea," Claire said.

"You already talked to Barry?" Kate asked, annoyance and disbelief edging into her voice.

"Kate?" Barry called from the doorway to his office. "Can I speak with you for a moment?"

Kate shot Claire a dirty look and stood up, making her way through the newsroom to Barry's office. He held the door open for her and ushered her inside before closing it behind her.

"Please, have a seat," he said, gesturing to the two battered chairs in front of his desk. Kate supposed they had once been nice but now the leather was old and cracked. She sat in one and Barry sat across from her in his desk chair. That, too, looked like it hadn't be updated in decades. Barry also looked like he might be in need of an update; his hair was thinning, his clothes were well worn, and he had suitcases under his eyes.

"So," Barry said, leaning forward on his desk, elbows resting on top of a tired yellow file folder. "Claire tells me that your uncle is pretty high ranking in the army."

"Yeah, he's a four-star general," Kate replied. She couldn't help the note of pride in her voice.

"Impressive," Barry said, nodding his head. "I imagine he'll be at Central Park today."

"Of course."

Barry waited for a moment, as if he expected her to say something else. She said nothing.

"Look, Kate, I'm going to cut to the chase. Can you call your uncle and use your press pass to get some exclusive coverage of this thing?"

"I don't know, I--" Kate started but Barry interrupted.

"No one else can have the access that you can. Of course, there'll be a press pen--I'll be there--but you could get right up next to the action. You could be one of the first people to see these aliens! And think of it--if the Eye got this level of exclusive coverage, I can't even begin to imagine what that could do for this paper--or your career."

Kate was quiet for a moment, considering his words.

"Look, Kate, I'm going to level with you. I know that the Eye has no prestige and I know this isn't exactly the type of job you imagined yourself in when you picked journalism as your major at, what, Vassar?"

"NYU."

"NYU, right. But if you can get this kind of exclusive story on the biggest event in human history, you could write your ticket anywhere. Every paper in the city would be begging you to work for them. Hell, if you wanted to branch into TV you could probably do that too. This could be everything for you," Barry said.

Kate didn't say anything and Barry sighed.

"Am I selfishly pushing this so the Eye hopefully won't constantly be on the verge of folding? Yes, obviously. But this could be big for you too."

Kate studied Barry for a moment and saw the puffy tiredness around his eyes, the beaten down way he carried himself. She wondered if he'd once been like her, optimistic and hopeful with big dreams of becoming someone important. She wondered when he'd given that up and resigned himself to running a third-rate newspaper.

"I guess I could call my uncle," Kate said slowly. Barry's face lit up. "But I'm not promising anything--he could say no."

"Of course, of course," Barry said. "But hey, maybe he'll at least give you an exclusive interview even if he can't get you up close and personal with the little green men, right?"

"Yeah, maybe," Kate said.

Barry clapped his hands together, a loud smack that signaled their meeting was over.

"Alright, great! Well why don't you go give him a call and then we'll take it from there," he said as he rose to his feet. Kate followed suit and left the office. Barry closed the door behind her and Kate saw Claire was already waiting for her in the newsroom.

"So?" Claire asked expectantly, her hands tightly laced in front of her body.

"So, I guess I'm going to call my uncle," Kate said, sounding less than enthused.

"What, no thank you for pushing you to take advantage of an amazing career opportunity?" Claire asked, dropping her hands as she raised an eyebrow. Kate could tell she was trying to make a joke but there was a hardness to her tone.

"Claire, I really don't appreciate you going over my head to talk to Barry about something like this. And there's no guarantee that I'm going to get an interview--like I told Barry, my uncle could say no. This is a big deal, he might not want his niece tagging along the first time aliens come to Earth."

"Whatever, you know Gerry will say yes," Claire said, rolling her eyes as she turned and walked back to her desk. Kate sighed and returned to her own desk, retrieving her cell phone from her bag. She left the newsroom and turned left down a small hallway. The walls were lined with framed copies of prominent front pages of the New York Eye, but none were particularly impressive. The Eye was always a few steps behind the other papers and most of their headlines sounded recycled from the bigger, more impressive news outlets. The hallway was, Kate thought, intended to highlight some of their best work, but she found it almost as depressing as the fake ficus in the lobby. The Great Hall of Mediocrity did little to brighten up the atmosphere of the Eye.

Kate entered the small break room at the end of the hall and, thankfully, found it empty. She stuck her head back out into the hallway to be sure Claire hadn't followed her, but saw no one. Kate ducked back into the break room and sat down at the small formica table that was always slightly sticky. Kate regularly wiped it off with a paper towel but no one else seemed to share her desire for a clean eating space. Except for perhaps Claire, but Claire usually worked through lunch, eating a salad at her desk as she researched stories and followed leads. The break room wasn't really Claire's scene as she was not exactly predisposed to water cooler chit chat unless she needed something from one of her co-workers. Claire wasn't rude, but she also wasn't likely to organize the company picnic. Kate looked down at her phone but instead of dialing, she thought about Claire. They'd been assigned as roommates during their freshman year by the gods of residence life at NYU and had stuck together ever since. Kate knew Claire could seem cold and standoffish to a lot of people, but Kate also knew how motivated Claire was. She, like Kate, had been raised by a single mother. Claire's mother had gotten pregnant at seventeen, in a horribly cliched story of a cheerleader getting knocked up by the quarterback of the football team. Claire's dad had tried to stick it out with them for a few years, but one night, when Claire was four, Claire's dad had tucked her into bed, read her an extra story, and then went out for cigarettes and never returned.

"The longest cigarette run ever recorded," Claire always quipped when she recounted the story.

"He didn't have to visit a convenience store in China, but I guess he missed the one around the corner," she'd say with a laugh. But Claire knew, of course, that her dad hadn't accidentally missed the convenience store around the corner and in actuality, had chosen to go as far away as possible. Claire's mother, left alone with a small child to care for alone, had done her best to make ends meet but they rarely did. As a result, Claire's mother had often searched for solace in a bottle, a search that never seemed to end. Claire once told Kate that from an early age, she decided she wasn't going to be like her mother. Her mother had been so reliant on her looks to get what she wanted, and all it had gotten her was knocked up with a resentful daughter.

Kate had only met Claire's mother once, when she and Claire had moved into the freshman dorm at NYU. Kate mostly remembered Claire's mother looking tired, with flat brown eyes and faded blonde hair. She must have been pretty once, that much Kate could see, but the years had taken that away from her. Claire's father must have been handsome, as Claire seemed to have collected the best aspects of each of her parents' looks. But Claire was constantly trying to prove she was more than just a pretty face, that she was more than her mother. Claire had needed extensive scholarships to cover the cost of her tuition at NYU and as a result, Claire had dedicated all of her free time to studying. Kate wasn't sure she'd ever seen Claire get anything less than an A on any assignment or test, but Kate had privately seen her cry from stress and fear of a low GPA that could cause her to lose her scholarships and, subsequently, her space at NYU. Kate had always assumed that this was where a lot of Claire's severity came from, but Kate didn't know if that was true or she had just tried too hard to analyze her best friend after taking an introductory psychology class at NYU.

Kate stood back up again in the break room, feeling too anxious to sit. Kate paced in front of the fridge and the small yellowing countertop, feeling a little like a caged panther at the zoo. She glanced at her bandaged hand and sighed before she finally dialed. The phone rang several times and for a moment, Kate wasn't sure if he'd answer or not.

"Harper speaking," her uncle said, his brisk voice filling the phone.

"Hey, Uncle Gerry!" Kate said, trying to sound cheerful as she checked the cabinets for a first aid kit. She finally found it in one of the bottom drawers, next to a few stray plastic forks.

"Katie!" he said, his voice softening. "How are you?"

"Good, good, and you?" she asked as she opened the kit and took out a large square gauze pad.

He sighed.

"Busy with everything that's going on today."

"Oh, I'm sorry," Katie apologized, ready to get off the phone as she opened the gauze's sterile packaging.

"No, no, I didn't mean it like that, I always have time for you. What's up, kiddo?"

"Oh. Well, I won't keep you, I just wanted to ask you something," she said, not wanting to ask for this favor as she unwrapped the pressure bandage from her apartment and tossed away the bloodstained toilet paper in the trash.

"Sure, what is it?" he asked.

"Well, you know about the whole spaceship thing," she said, wincing more at the obviousness of her statement than the sharp pain in her hand when she ripped open an alcohol wipe and rubbed it against the cut.

"Yes, Katie, I'm aware."

"Right. So my boss wanted me to see if there was any way you could get me up close to the landing or in for an exclusive interview," Kate said quickly, all in one breath.

"There's going to be a press pen," he said slowly. "I can be sure you get in there, would that work?"

"I actually already have access to that," she said, desperately wanting this conversation to be over. "But my boss wanted to see if there was any way I could get an exclusive, something closer than that. Maybe an interview with you or someone else high up?" Kate placed the sterile gauze square on her hand and rewrapped the bandage, securing it snugly to her wrist.

"I don't know, Katie," Gerry said. "I don't really like to throw my weight around like that. And besides, we don't know how safe these aliens are. Your mom would kill me if I put you in any kind of danger and I'd never be able to forgive myself is something happened to you."

"Didn't you say that based on the ship's behavior thus far that it's likely they're peaceful? And isn't vice president going to be there? You wouldn't risk having him there if it weren't safe, right?"

"But you're my niece," Gerry said.

Kate's heart sank. The silence hung on the phone for a long beat and then Gerry sighed.

"Alright, Katie, I'll make it happen. Get to the West 67th Street entrance at 7:00, I'll leave word to make sure they let you in. My aide, Major Ben Anderson, will meet you there."

Kate felt an enormous wave of relief wash over her.

"Thank you so much, Uncle Gerry, I appreciate this so much. I really owe you one."

"Don't be ridiculous, you don't owe me anything. Tell you what--in exchange, let me buy you dinner after you write your big article."

Kate laughed.

"That hardly seems fair to you!" she protested.

"It's more than fair, it makes me happy to do that for you. What? Hang on, Katie," he said. Kate heard him pull the phone away from his ear, discussing something with whomever had just interrupted the call. "Katie, I'm sorry, I have to go. I'll see you tonight."

"Okay. Thank you again!"

"Bye, kiddo."

Kate hung up and stared at her phone for a minute. She was actually going to get in up close and personal with the aliens. This was really happening! Then a thought hit her and she groaned.

"Damn it!" she exclaimed, her voice filling the empty break room. She'd actually have to thank Claire for interfering.

That evening, at 6:45, Kate approached the West 67th Street entrance to Central Park. She'd agonized over her clothes, uncertain of the appropriate thing to wear to meet aliens, and had finally settled on something that made her feel like like an international news correspondent or at least a somewhat responsible adult: a white button up shirt with high-waisted black pants. Simple, professional, and inoffensive. Sure, she was regretting wearing pants in the hot New York evening, but at least she'd had the sense to wear flat shoes, despite Claire's protestations that she should wear heels. The street was already packed with people and it took a lot of maneuvering for Kate to get through the crowd, her bag bumping against her hip. The entrance was heavily blockaded by both police officers and soldiers and Kate hoped her uncle had remembered to leave word for her to get in.

"Excuse me," Kate said, reaching out to tap the nearest soldier on the shoulder.

"Ma'am, I'm going to need you to stay back, there's no admittance past this point," he said tersely, pulling his shoulder out of reach.

Kate wondered if being 22 qualified you as being old enough to be a "ma'am" rather than a "miss."

"My uncle said he'd leave word--" Kate started to say but the soldier cut her off.

"Ma'am, I don't care who you're uncle is, you're not getting in here," the soldier interjected, eyeing her press badge. *Again with the ma'am*, Kate thought. "You're welcome to head over to the press pen if you'd like, but you're not getting through me."

"Are you Kate Porter?" another man in uniform asked as he approached them. In spite of herself, Kate couldn't help but be momentarily taken aback by his handsome face and rich chestnut skin.

"Yes, I am," she answered.

"I'm Major Anderson, General Harper sent me over here to make sure you didn't have any problems getting past security," he explained, not even bothering to glance at the soldier to whom Kate had just been speaking.

"Wait, are you General Harper's niece?" the soldier asked Kate incredulously.

"Yes, she is," Major Anderson said.

"Yes, sir," the soldier replied, remembering his rank. Kate eyed Major Anderson, slightly annoyed.

Handsome or not, she didn't enjoy being spoken for, especially after Claire had already gone over her head once today.

"Yes, I'm General Harper's niece," Kate told the soldier. "I can speak for myself," she said to Major Anderson. He raised an eyebrow at her but didn't comment further on the matter.

"Let's get you to your uncle," he said instead, turning to lead her into the park. Kate followed him past scores of heavily armed military forces until they were just beside the large, roped off area in Sheep Meadow. She looked up and saw the spaceship, round and large and imposing. It was lower than it had been this morning, although still above the tree line.

"Wait here, I'll go get him for you," Major Anderson said. Kate was about to protest that she could get him herself until she noticed her uncle talking to the vice president of the United States and decided that maybe that was one conversation she didn't want to interrupt. She nodded, and as Major Anderson walked off, she returned her gaze to the ship. When she'd first heard about the spaceship, Kate had been expecting, on some level, something cartoonish, like a round ship with a dome on the top beaming up a cow in the middle of a cornfield. Up to this point, her experience with spaceships had been limited to cartoons and science fiction movie franchises. But now, faced with an actual spaceship, it looked both familiar and like nothing she had expected. It was round, that much was true, but it didn't have a dome on top. It was thick, mucher thicker than she'd expected. If pressed for a comparison, Kate thought it looked more like a metallic slice of a tree trunk than anything else, but instead of floating over a farm, it was hovering over New York City. There weren't any cows around although Kate supposed that in Sheep Meadow, one of the spectators might be as good as any cow for a curious extraterrestrial looking to probe a life force from planet Earth.

"Katie."

Kate turned to see her uncle walking towards her with Major Anderson at his elbow. She grinned and stepped to meet him as he wrapped her in a hug, his pins and medals that adorned his uniform pressing against her cheek.

"Any problems at the gate?"

Kate glanced at Major Anderson but his expression was passive and unreadable.

"Nope, no problems," she said, looking back to her uncle. Kate's glance at Major Anderson hadn't gone unnoticed by the general, but he didn't mention it.

"What happened to your hand?" the general asked, his eyes immediately drawn to the bandage on Kate's left arm.

"Oh, it's nothing," Kate said. "I was jogging this morning and I tripped and cut my hand on a break in the sidewalk."

"Did you see a doctor?" Gerry asked.

"No, it's fine. It's just a scratch," Kate insisted.

"Did you clean it properly? Because if you cut it on a New York City sidewalk, there's a chance you picked up some kind of super bacteria that's resistant to antibiotics. The ground in this city is disgusting."

"How much longer until it touches down?" Kate asked, changing the subject as she pulled a notebook and pen out of her bag.

"It should start the final descent in just a few minutes," General Harper said, looking up at the ship.

"Have you had any direct contact with the aliens yet?"

The general shook his head.

"Not yet, all the information we have has been gathered from our own instruments, tracking and charting the ship."

"But you don't think they're dangerous?" Kate asked, scribbling notes on her pad.

"No, although I'm still cautious. Realistically, if they wanted to do something to attack us, they would've done it already since they've been over New York City for days. I still don't think it's a great idea to have the vice president here," the general said, glancing over towards the vice president and the secretary of state, "but that's not my decision. Don't write that," he said suddenly, realizing Kate's pen was flying over the paper.

"I promise, none of your insubordination will make it into my report," Kate said with a grin.

"It better not, young lady," he said warningly, but he was smiling. "Smartass," he added.

"It's why I'm your favorite niece," Kate said.

"The fact that you're my only niece is beside the point," General Harper said.

"Sir," Major Anderson interjected. "Sorry to interrupt, but . . ." he trailed off, pointing up to the sky. The ship was starting to descend a little faster. The general turned and started barking orders at everyone, getting them into position. The soldiers stood at attention, guns and tanks trained on the descending ship.

"Doesn't really look like a peaceful reception," Kate murmured to Major Anderson, who was still standing at her side.

"Just covering our bases," he said as he glanced over at Kate and noticed her gaze directed towards the weaponry.

"Sure, of course," Kate said.

Major Anderson returned his attention to the ship. Once everyone was in place, the general returned to stand by Kate and Ben. The three of them looked up at the spaceship together as it made its way down into Central Park. The general put an arm around his niece and hugged her briefly before returning to his professional, militaristic posture.

"Christ, it looks like a bad B-movie," General Harper muttered to Kate, who suppressed a laugh as the spaceship touched down on Earth.

Chapter 2

The spaceship landed very gently, almost silently, on the grass. It towered over Kate as she stood with her uncle and Major Anderson. She couldn't even hear the crowd in the background and the city felt hushed, truly quiet for what was likely the first time in its existence. They waited for what felt like an eternity, but in reality was probably only a couple minutes, before the sound of mechanics whirring within the spaceship could be heard. A panel in the exterior of the ship moved aside, sliding inside of itself to reveal a large, handleless silver door. A moment later, the silver door opened and a bright white light beamed out from inside the ship. As Kate's eyes adjusted, she began to make out two figures standing in the doorway. One was a little taller than the other and they looked somewhat human although she couldn't be sure with the backlight masking their features. The beings slowly exited the spaceship together and as they stepped out onto the grass, the park lights began to illuminate their faces. Their skin was very pale, almost completely colorless, and they wore dark blue jumpsuits, tightly fitted to their humanoid forms. Kate couldn't see them especially well from where she stood but she could see that the taller one had closely cropped dark hair, not unlike Major Anderson, and the shorter one had carefully combed short blue hair. The shorter alien turned its head, curiously, as if it were looking for someone. Its eyes met and held Kate's and they gazed at each other for several long moments. General Harper refused to break his stance, but he felt his heart rate quicken as he watched the alien watch his niece. The alien's eyes were slightly larger than a human's, and the brilliant blue color was unlike anything Kate had seen before. The nose was slim and delicate and the alien's ears were flush against the side of its head. There was some sort of line curving on the alien's head behind its ear, although from this distance Kate couldn't quite tell what it was. Kate and the alien stared, studying one another as the alien tilted its head to one side. It was then that Kate realized the alien didn't have a mouth. Where one should've been was only an empty, smooth stretch of skin above a strong jawline. The taller alien continued towards the waiting vice president. The blue haired alien glanced at its companion, as if it had suddenly remembered why they were there, and followed.

"Stay here," General Harper murmured to Major Anderson before he left Kate's side, walking over slowly to join the vice president. The general felt a little relieved that the alien's attention was diverted back to the vice president because, if he was honest, he found the vice president far more disposable than his niece.

Kate watched the way the aliens walked, admiring their precise, elegant posture and their slow steps. They reminded her of dancers with their smooth, fluid movements. Kate wasn't much of a dancer, although she vaguely remembered taking some ballet classes when she was little. She never really went out dancing, hadn't since her junior year of college, but when she had she'd always felt awkward and stiff on the dance floor. Claire, naturally, had never accompanied her to a club. Now, she and Claire would sometimes stop at a wine bar near their apartment (for one glass only, Claire never permitted herself a second) but there was, thankfully, no dancing at that particular bar.

The aliens only took a few stops before they stopped and raised their hands. Kate noticed that they only had three fingers on each hand which vaguely reminded her of a cartoon character. She felt an inappropriate giggle expand in her chest like a bubble. Kate had no idea why this was funny because it obviously wasn't--at all. But the laugh was there all the same. She bent her head to write a note on her pad and the giggle escaped out of her nose in rapid bursts of air as she wrote. Major Anderson glared at her out of the corner of her eye, which sobered her up a little when she noticed him, but the nervous energy was still there, threatening to escape at this very inopportune time.

The taller alien began to gesture with its hands. It paused and looked expectantly at the vice president and General Harper. The alien appeared to be trying to use some kind of sign language, but a quick conference with the translator who was standing just outside the ring of secret service agents surrounding the vice president didn't seem the clarify the situation. Kate couldn't hear what the translator was saying from where she stood, but she could tell he had no idea what the alien was trying to say as the translator shrugged his shoulders. The alien tried again, repeating the hand motions, but the message remained unclear. The alien glanced back at its companion and Kate could see the alien's brow furrowed in frustration. Although Kate couldn't hear anything, it appeared that the two aliens were having some sort of silent conversation, each reacting in turn to words no one else could hear. Kate looked over at her uncle, who stood, shifting his eyes from the aliens to the vice president, to her, and then back again to the aliens. She knew that even though he'd posted the major with her, he wasn't going to fully relinquish her care to anyone else.

Kate thought, for what felt like the millionth time in her life, that it was a shame Gerry had never had kids of his own. Her mom once told her that Gerry was married to the military, but Kate still wished things had been different for him. She'd asked him once, when she was about ten, why he didn't have any kids of his own.

"Don't need 'em," he'd said with a smile, gently tugging on the end of her ponytail. "With a niece like you, you keep me plenty busy, kiddo."

Kate supposed he really had been like a father to her, especially since her dad died when she was four. A drunk driver ran a red light and plowed into the side of her dad's car, hitting it with such force that it had scrunched the metal door as if it had been made of paper. Kate's father had died en route to the hospital but the drunk driver had sustained only minor cuts and bruises. Such was the way these things always seemed to go.

Kate had seen the car a couple days after the accident. She had gone with her mom to the impound lot to meet the "claims guy." Kate had thought her mother had said "clams" and wondered why a car would have anything to do with a clam. She'd expected her mom to drive to the beach, but instead they drove to a parking lot next to another fenced parking lot of beat up cars. The day had been cool, only two weeks before Halloween, and Kate's mom had instructed her to stay in the car. Gerry had met them there, pulling his car into the parking spot beside theirs.

"Jesus, Miranda, you brought Kate?" Kate had heard her uncle say as he got out of his car.

"I couldn't leave her at home. I--" her mother had started to say before she stopped, her shoulders shaking. Kate couldn't see her mother's face from where she sat in the backseat but she'd watched her uncle pull his sister in for a long hug.

"Hey, Katie," Gerry had said after he'd let go of Kate's mother, leaning down to open the backdoor to see her.

"Hi, Uncle Gerry!" Kate had said. "Do you want to play 'I Spy'?"

He'd smiled at her, a little sadly.

"Not now, honey, I have to help your mom with something. But can I play with you later?"

"Sure," Kate had said. "Are you here to see the clams guy?"

"Something like that," Gerry had said. "I need you to stay here in the car while I help your mom, can you do that for me? We'll just be right over there so if you need us, you can just open the door and shout, okay?"

"Okay," Kate had said.

Gerry had shut the door and Kate remembered watching her mother and uncle walk around to the entrance of the impound lot to talk to the man in the booth. She'd wondered if he was the one with the clams. The man in the booth let them inside and shortly after, they were joined by another man, shorter than her uncle, but skinnier, like the pipe cleaners they used sometimes at school for art projects. He'd led them over to one of the first cars in the lot. Kate had watched through the chainlink fence as her mother started crying, with Gerry standing stiffly beside her. The car was dark green like Kate's father's car, but Kate had been sure it wasn't the same vehicle. Her father's car wasn't all squished and crumpled like a discarded t-shirt on the bathroom floor. And yet, in spite of all of Kate's convictions that this wasn't her father's car, he never came home again. Neither did his car.

Two weeks later, when Kate's mother had still been unable to get out of bed, Gerry had taken Kate trick or treating around her neighborhood. She'd worn the princess costume her father had bought her a few days before the accident and everyone told her what a pretty princess she made. They'd all told Gerry what a beautiful daughter he had and Kate had corrected each of them petulantly until the last house. An older lady with white hair had given her two pieces of candy instead of just one, winking at her as she dropped them in Kate's candy bag.

"You're lucky to have such a nice daddy to take you around tonight, your highness," the lady had said, smiling at Kate. But Kate hadn't smiled back. Instead, she'd burst into tears.

"He's not my daddy! My daddy's gone! He's never coming back!" Kate had screamed before she whirled around and ran away from the house towards the sidewalk. As she ran, she could hear Gerry start to apologize and now, thinking back, Kate assumed Gerry had told the lady about her father, but she didn't know if there'd been time for him to do that and run after her. He'd caught up to her just as Kate turned to run down the street, catching her arm before she could go any further. Kate had cried, dropping her candy bag on the pavement.

"It's okay, Katie," Gerry had said, pulling her close to him as other parents and their costumed children gave them a polite, wide berth on the sidewalk. Kate had cried into his shoulder until the great, heaving sobs had finally slowed into little gasps and sighs as Kate ran out of tears. He'd picked her up then, careful to retrieve her candy bag as well, and had carried her home, her face buried in his neck. He had smelled faintly of sweat and soap and Kate had felt safe.

Major Anderson touched Kate on the elbow, interrupting her thoughts. He tilted his head, indicating to her that he was going to move closer to the general and the vice president. She nodded. The major moved slowly, inching closer to General Harper. The vice president cleared his throat and the two aliens stopped their silent conversation and looked over at him. The vice president looked nervous, but straightened his shoulders, looking as if he were attempting to exude a confidence he didn't seem to feel.

"Hello," the vice president said, his voice sounding more even than Kate had expected. "Welcome."

The introduction sounded awkward but Kate didn't think she could blame him--it's not like there was a rule book with guidelines on how to properly greet extraterrestrials for the first time.

"My name is Martin Harris. I'm the vice president of the United States of America," the vice president said, seemingly due to a lack of anything else to say. The aliens stared at him before looking back to each other and the shorter one shrugged its shoulders, uncomprehending. The two aliens turned back to the vice president and Kate slowly pulled her cell phone out of her bag. She wasn't entirely sure she was supposed to have it in the cordoned off park, but whether or not it was allowed, it was in her hand. When she'd put it in her bag before heading to the Central Park, she'd half expected it to get confiscated but no one had done a search of her bag. Probably because as General Harper's niece, escorted by Major Anderson, Kate hadn't seemed like a big security threat. She took a step towards the aliens as she opened the camera app on her smartphone. No one else would have a photo like this, it would be the perfect thing to accompany her article. And besides, Kate could practically hear Claire's chastising voice if Kate didn't get a picture. General Harper noticed Kate's movements and tried to lock eyes with her. She purposely didn't look at him. Kate didn't want to disobey her uncle, but she also didn't want to miss this once in a lifetime opportunity. Kate crept forward, trying to get closer for a better shot. She edged sideways, trying to frame the vice president between the two aliens. Kate wasn't much of a photographer, and while she had grandiose ideas in her head about composition and lighting, she really just hoped it would be in focus. She wasn't exactly known for taking the sharpest photos and had, on occasion, put her finger partially over the lens or unwittingly cropped out someone's head.

The taller alien looked to the blue haired alien and it appeared that they were once again conversing, although still neither of them made a sound. The taller one nodded to the shorter alien who took a small device out of his pocket. The soldiers around the perimeter of the ship instantly straightened up, tightening their hold on their guns, their muscles tense and ready. The shorter alien noticed this and looked around, slightly confused. It glanced back, its blue eyes finding Kate again, and it seemed to her that it was looking for some sort of confirmation or explanation from her. Its eyes, even from that short distance, looked expectant and ready for an answer, although it didn't seem surprised or alarmed by her change in location. Kate wasn't sure what it wanted her to say or do so she chose the safest course of action--nothing. She stood completely still, her phone poised and ready. The shorter alien glanced down at the device in its hand and Kate tapped the screen of her phone. Just as Kate's phone flashed, the alien pushed the button on the device and, suddenly, the entire city went black.

The park was immediately thrown into chaos. The only light came from the spaceship and in that bright glow, Kate saw the secret service agents dive around the vice president and hurry him away, quickly swallowed by the darkness. Screams came from the crowds outside the park and General Harper was desperately trying to maintain some kind of order in Sheep Field.

"Hold your fire!" He shouted to the soldiers, cupping his hands around his mouth to try to carry his voice over the confusion. "Hold your fire!"

The aliens looked to each other, startled by this sudden change in events, and edged closer to one another. Kate felt frozen to where she stood, her phone still held out in front of her, too terrified to put it down, let alone move.

"Do they have weapons?" someone shouted from a distance.

"A weapon?" someone else shouted from the opposite direction.

"Weapons! They have weapons!" another voice screamed. The air exploded into a thundering display as the gunfire flashed like thousands of tiny fireflies. Kate was suddenly knocked to the ground and she felt the air in her lungs forced out in a rough heave. She realized Major Anderson had tackled her and was pinning her down on the grass.

"Stay down!" he shouted in her ear, only somewhat audible over the shots. He crawled back towards General Harper who, in the light of the ship, was frantically gesturing to Major Anderson to stay put. The spaceship light suddenly turned off and what little illumination they had had was stolen from them. Kate could hear more people screaming as the gunfire continued and she dropped her phone in the grass, covering her ears with her hands. Oh God, what had she done? She squeezed her eyes shut, praying everything would stop, wishing that she had never let Claire or Barry convince her to do this. She should've been in the press pen like everyone else.

Kate felt someone grab her arm and roughly pull her up. She thought it was Major Anderson until she realized that the hand holding her only had three fingers. She screamed.

"Katie!" General Harper yelled. "Katie, where are you?"

"Gerry!" she tried to scream but she was pulled into the ship and the last of her uncle's name was cut off by a thundering explosion.

Chapter 3

"Kate!" the general shouted, desperately shining a flashlight around the grass. "Kate!"

Even if she'd been there, there's no way she would've been able to hear him over the confusion that stampeded through the park. The gunfire had ceased in the wake of the explosion, but the terrified cries of the city remained, chorusing into the night.

"Ben!" General Harper finally called instead.

"Sir," Ben replied, already at his elbow.

"What the hell happened?" the general barked. "Where is my niece?"

"I--I don't know," Ben stammered. "I got her down on the ground and told her to stay put. I was heading back towards you when the explosion happened, and--"

The general walked away in the middle of Ben's explanation, not caring to hear the rest. He scanned the ground with his flashlight, looking for something, anything. Then, he saw it in the grass: Kate's phone. He recognized the phone case, the one that looked like newsprint. He'd bought it for her when she got hired by that newspaper. What was it called? The New York Sky? Eye? He shook his head as he bent down and reached for the phone. It didn't matter. When he turned the phone over, the screen had a deep crack in it across the top left corner, but otherwise it seemed okay. As the shouting and running in the park continued around him, General Harper momentarily ignored it and clicked a button to light up the screen. Kate didn't have a password on her phone, which seemed ridiculous to Gerry. He'd told her to add one a dozen times and, as a member of the press, she should really know better. However, at that moment, he was grateful for her lackadaisical security. He didn't want to have to hand her phone over to the tech unit to unlock it. He swiped the phone's screen and it opened back up to the last application, the camera.

"Sir," Ben said, at his side once more, holding a flashlight of his own. General Harper ignored him and clicked on the image in the corner. It filled the screen and the general studied the photo. The vice president was framed between the two aliens while the shorter of the two looked at something in its hand. The general tried to zoom in on the photo but he couldn't quite tell what the alien had in its odd, three-fingered hand. Whatever it was, the general was sure it was what had caused the EMP.

"Sir," Ben said again. General Harper finally acknowledged him with a glance in his direction. "Sir, the Secretary of Defense is on the phone," Ben said, holding up the satellite phone as evidence. "You're needed at the Pentagon."

The general glanced around the in darkness, flashlights still bouncing around the black city. He sighed, exasperated. He hated to leave the park, but he knew he didn't have a choice.

"Find me Lieutenant General Fauss," General Harper ordered. "She can handle the park and get this shit show under control."

"Yes, sir," Ben said before he disappeared into the darkness once more. General Harper looked down at Kate's phone again, examining the photo one more time before clicking off the screen and tucking it into his pocket. He wasn't sure where Kate was, but he was not prepared to consider the possibilities, not right then. General Harper looked up at the sky, hoping to see the spaceship. The ship wasn't there, but he did see the glittering lights of thousands of stars blanketed above New York City. Gerry had loved stars as a kid and had even wanted to become an astronomer for a while. However, his father hadn't been too keen on the idea.

"Whaddaya want to do, just stare at the sky all day?" his father had asked. Although he was only thirteen at the time, Gerry had thought it wise to not correct his father and point out that as an astronomer, he'd need to look at the night sky to see anything.

"I want to learn more about space," Gerry had said instead. "What if there are other planets out there with aliens? Wouldn't that be cool to meet them?" he asked.

"You want to spend your time chasing some fictional little green men?" his father had asked. "Gerald, be serious. You can read a science fiction book in your free time or watch a movie, but remember, it's just that--fiction. You have to do something that actually matters in this world and staring at the sky just isn't that important."

Gerry had wanted to tell him that he did think staring at the sky and the stars was important because science was important and he wanted to learn more, to see more. But he hadn't said anything of the sort.

"Yes, sir," Gerry had said. His father had nodded, the tilt of his head signaling the end of the discussion. The final end of that particular topic, as it would turn out, never to be revisited. So although Gerry had wanted to study the stars, he'd joined the army instead. Doing something that mattered. Now, the only stars he saw were the ones on his uniform. Except for now. Gerry was momentarily taken aback by the rare sight before he looked away and, using his flashlight, headed towards the park's exit. Once again, doing what mattered.

On the plane to Arlington, the general sat alone by a window. The vice president sat several rows ahead, equally uncommunicative, although far more nervous than the general. If anyone tapped him on the arm, the vice president would jump, his eyes scanning around him for danger. Everyone quickly picked up on this and stopped touching him. General Harper glanced across at the aisle at Major Anderson who was staring at his hands. Ben hadn't said a word since they boarded the plane and the general wasn't sure how he felt about him at that moment. He wasn't a bad kid. In fact, he was a great soldier. General Harper depended on him and trusted him implicitly and he felt almost paternal towards Ben. And yet . . . he had been in charge of Kate. Kate was gone. It was difficult to say what "gone" meant at the moment, but the semantics didn't really matter just then. The general looked back out the window. He wasn't sure what to say to Ben, if there was even anything to say, so he said nothing.

The secure meeting room in the bowels of the Pentagon was in complete chaos. Each side of the room was shouting to be heard, the cacophonous voices creating a migraine-inducing din. General Harper's thoughts, however, were turned inward. He couldn't stop thinking about Central Park and the crater that the ship had left behind. He hoped fervently that Kate hadn't gone out that way in an explosion, but, then again, the alternative was that she was on the ship with the aliens. The general wasn't sure which option he preferred.

"Alright, everybody, now shut up for just a minute!" a large man bellowed, his voice effectively silencing the room. Colonel Wyatt Hascomb hailed from Dallas, Texas and his waistline had seen its fair share of barbecues. "Now, listen up," he said in his southern drawl. "We're not going to get anything done by hollering at each other so we need to talk this thing out. We've got every major world leader on the phone looking for some goddamn answers and we need to hurry up and figure out what those answers are."

General Harper glanced over at President Roman Wolff, who looked surprisingly calm amidst the chaos of the planet's predicament. The president was leaning back in his chair, one leg crossed to rest his ankle on his knee, and his elbow sat heavily on the arm of the chair, one finger at his temple while he rested his chin on his hand. President Wolff had been quietly watching the mayhem in the room unfold, not offering any of his own opinions, just observing. Waiting. General Harper remembered how during the election, the president's detractors had labeled him a "Wolff in sheep's clothing" and he could see what they meant. The man was almost unnerving in his measured self-control as he casually watched the world fall to pieces with his dark eyes. But the general was familiar with that level of self-control, he'd been exercising it himself for decades, and so he put on his own mask as a slightly calmer discussion than before resumed.

"I think we need to take militaristic action and fast," the Secretary of Defense said, sitting up straighter in her chair. "If they blow up Central Park, we need to show them that we're not going to stand for it."

"Is that really wise?" another woman asked. "I don't think we have enough information to make that call."

"The world is waiting for us to act," the Secretary of State said. "Other countries are waiting for us to take the lead on this and if we make the wrong move, it'll compromise our standing in international affairs."

"There's not going to be any goddamn international affairs if we don't have a planet!" the Colonel shouted, banging his fist on the table as he stood.

"What was that about not hollering, Colonel?" the general asked coolly.

Colonel Hascomb made a face but he lowered his voice, although he remained standing.

"North Korea has been looking for an excuse to launch its entire payload of nukes and for once, I think those fascist idiots are right."

"Okay, that's enough," General Harper interrupted. "Let's all just step back for a second," General Harper continued, not wanting the room to erupt in another verbal explosion. "First of all, they didn't blow up Central Park. There was an explosion, but it just resulted in a crater--Central Park is still there. There's no need to start some kind of "Remember Central Park" memorial fund. Second of all, we still don't know who or what we're dealing with here and without that information, we'd be stumbling into God knows what with our guns blazing, which is just plain stupid. Third, we're tracking the ship and it's moving up and out of our weapons' range anyway."

"Plus, there's Kate," Ben said quietly. The entire room's attention shifted to him and the air thickened.

"What?" the general asked, quietly and evenly.

"Kate could be on the ship," Ben said.

General Harper took a breath but said nothing.

"Who the hell is Kate?" Colonel Hascomb asked, annoyed.

General Harper cleared his throat.

"My niece. She disappeared after the EMP and we have reason to believe she might be on the ship."

"Is she the idiot who took the picture?" Colonel Hascomb asked. General Harper said nothing but slowly rose up from his chair, glaring at the colonel. The two men locked eyes and the seconds ticked by in the uncomfortable silence of the room.

After what felt like an agonizingly long time, Colonel Hascomb slowly sank down into his chair.

"Sorry," the colonel said quietly.

General Harper sat back down.

"Look, Harper, I'm sorry about your niece. Really, I am. But I think we need to fire on the spaceship," the vice president said, speaking up for the first time. Gerry looked at him and saw that the vice president's hands were shaking. The vice president caught the general looking at his hands and he put them down in his lap, out of sight. "I was there, looking them right in their big, weird eyes, and I don't think they're here for a slumber party."

"I understand, sir, but I was there too," General Harper said. "None of us know why they're here--we simply don't have the information."

"We also still don't have power within a seven block radius of Central Park," the Secretary of Defense said. "There's a hole in the middle of the park, there was a massive firefight when everyone started shooting off their guns, the hospitals are full of people who were hit by stray bullets."

"You can't blame the aliens for the gunfire," the general interrupted. "They didn't shoot anybody."

"Who should we blame for the gunfire?" the Secretary of State asked General Harper. He could tell what she was implying but he didn't respond to it.

"You're right, general, they didn't shoot anybody. But they caused the EMP that led to the shootings," the Secretary of Defense said. "People are scared and they're looking for a sign that we're strong and are going to protect them."

"So we just blow them up out of fear?" General Harper asked, raising an eyebrow. "And what if they get out of range, then what do we do?"

"That's why we need to do something now!" the vice president insisted, his voice rising. "By firing on them now, we take out the threat before they have a chance to escape."

"What about Kate?" Major Anderson interjected.

"Ben," General Harper hissed in a tone that, in no uncertain terms, told him to shut up.

"The needs of the many outweigh the needs of the few," the vice president quipped. The Secretary of Defense and Colonel Hascomb nodded in agreement.

"You're willing to sacrifice the life of an American civilian out of fear?" Ben asked, sounding increasingly angry.

"Watch it, Major," the vice president said, narrowing his eyes. "And yes, I am willing to make that sacrifice if it means preserving the rest of humanity and life as we know it."

"What if there are more?" General Harper asked. "What if this is only one ship out of a hundred? A thousand?"

"Then we prepare for goddamn intergalactic battle," Colonel Hascomb said. "These things can't just come in here and do whatever they want to our planet."

General Harper barely resisted the urge to roll his eyes.

"And how exactly do you propose we defend ourselves in a 'goddamn intergalactic battle'?" the general asked. "These aliens have mastered interplanetary travel--they clearly have the upper hand. Sheer patriotism isn't going to be enough to take down an alien fleet with far more advanced technologies than we have in our possession."

"I'd rather go out with my guns blazing on my own terms than as a submissive pet to some alien race," Colonel Hascomb retorted.

This time, General Harper didn't resist the urge to roll his eyes. The colonel ignored him and he and the Secretary of Defense launched into a discussion about how best to obliterate a spaceship. Other voices joined in, the volume rising once more. General Harper looked over at Ben who looked furious. Gerry glanced down and saw Ben clenching and unclenching a fist in his lap.

"I'm going to do everything I can to get her back," General Harper said quietly as he leaned over to Ben's ear. "I know you will too."

Major Anderson didn't say anything, but he nodded. General Harper sat back in his chair and surveyed the room, now consumed with the logistics of blowing up a space craft. President Wolff leaned over to the general.

"Do you feel like the possibility of your niece being on board is clouding your judgment?" President Wolff asked General Harper. The general's stomach twisted but he kept his face impassive He knew this was a test and he didn't hesitate to answer.

"No. I understand what's at stake here and that, sometimes, sacrifices are necessary," General Harper replied, matching the president's hushed voice. He'd never lied to the commander in chief before in his life. The president watched him for a moment, his expression unreadable.

"What do you think the best course of action is?" President Wolff asked.

"I think we need to wait until we have more information," the general said. "We know so little about these aliens and, realistically, they're probably already out of range by now. Making a rash decision while emotions are so high would be extremely foolish. If this ship reaches out to us again, it could be our one chance to successfully navigate peaceful communication before the situation possibly escalates in a very violent way."

The president stared at him for a moment, thinking.

"I agree," he said. He stood suddenly and all the side conversations in the room stopped as suddenly as if the president had hit the mute button on a remote.

"We hold our fire until we have more information," President Wolff said. "Now, let's get the power back on in New York and I believe we should be expecting some visitors in D.C." he concluded before smoothly exiting the room. In a flash, the Secretaries of Defense and State were on his heels along with Colonel Hascomb. General Harper watched the trio leave the room, their voices echoing and receding in the hallway. General Harper stayed seated as the rest of the participants in the room rose and left. He heard one of them mention prepping gallons of coffee for the night ahead. It wasn't until that moment that Gerry realized how tired he actually was. The adrenaline of the past few hours had drained his body, but there was no rest for those trying to prevent a space war. The general looked around the now empty conference room and sighed. He knew this was only one of many battles he was about to fight tonight and he had to get it together if he was going to keep everyone in one piece.

"Sir?"

The general looked over towards the door where Ben was now standing, holding a notepad.

"Yes?" he asked.

"You have several messages."

Harper gave a tired laugh.

"Yeah, I imagine I do. Just give me the list, I'll start working on them on the way over to the meeting," he said, holding out his hand. But Ben didn't give him the paper immediately. "Is there something else?"

"Six of the messages are from your sister," Ben said. The general let his hand drop.

"Shit."

"Yeah," Ben agreed. "The last call came in ten minutes ago, she wants you to call her immediately."

The general leaned back in his chair, pinching the bridge of his nose. He rubbed his eyes until he saw stars, much uglier than the ones he'd seen in the park. Gerry kept his eyes closed for another moment. He had no idea what he was going to tell Miranda. His sister had been through enough in her life, from losing Tom in that car crash to her current ongoing battle with breast cancer. General Harper did not want to add a dead or abducted daughter to that list. He opened his eyes, staring blankly across the room. She'd been downgraded to stage four last week, but Miranda had made him swear not to tell Kate. Kate knew about the cancer, of course, but she didn't know how bad it was. Miranda always tried to put on a happy face around her daughter, but she knew Kate wasn't stupid. Gerry was sure Kate noticed the pain on her mother's face, her increasing frailty. But Kate hadn't explicitly asked her uncle what her mother's cancer status was so Gerry hadn't volunteered any information. He didn't like lying to his niece, even by omission, but he did as his sister had asked him. The woman had a death sentence, it was the least Gerry could do for her. But now, if Kate really was gone, it might not even matter that he'd kept the secret from his niece. The general felt tears begin to prick the corners of his eyes but he forced them back, sitting stoically until he couldn't feel them anymore.

"Sir?" Ben asked quietly. General Harper glanced over, he'd forgotten Ben was still there.

"I'll call her," the general said. Ben dutifully held out the list and General Harper scanned the names, all of them familiar, all of them urgent. "Give me a minute, I'll meet you downstairs," he said to Ben who nodded and left, tactfully closing the door behind him. The general took Kate's phone out of his pocket and set it on the table in front of him before he pulled out his own phone. He set the two devices side by side and looked at them. Their phones were the same make and model, formerly twins before the crack had sprouted on Kate's screen. He wondered who had stepped on it. Not that it mattered, but he still wondered who had been close enough to Kate before she . . . well, he didn't want to think about that. The general took a deep breath, picked up his own phone, and dialed his sister. She answered midway through the first ring.

"Miranda, it's me . . . Yes, I'm fine . . . Katie is . . . Look, I can tell you what I know. It's not much but it's all we have right now. I--" he started but his voice cracked. He cleared his throat, trying to force back the emotions he didn't want to face. Suddenly, he was overwhelmed, like an ocean wave crashing over his head and he started sobbing into the phone, dropping his head down. "I don't know . . . Miranda, I don't know . . . I'm sorry. I should've . . . no, it is, this is my fault," he said before he lost the ability to form words and he simply cried with his sister, unable to do anything else.

Chapter 4

Kate was reading in her bedroom when the doorbell rang. The chime bing-bonged through the house and sounded perversely loud in contrast to the silence that permeated every room. She didn't know who it was and she didn't care--she didn't want to see anyone. Not tonight. Kate turned another page in her book but she couldn't really focus on the words. They may have been hieroglyphic squiggles for all the sense they were making to her at the moment. There was a tap on the door.

"Kate?" she heard her mother call. "There's someone here to see you."

Kate looked up, confused. She was ten years old and didn't exactly get a lot of visitors, especially not on a Friday night.

"Who is it?" she called back.

The door opened a crack and Kate saw her mother's face peering at her.

"Can we come in?" her mother asked.

"I guess," Kate said.

Her mother stepped aside and Kate saw Gerry standing in the hallway, wearing his blue dress uniform. The medals shone when the light from Kate's bedroom hit them and she noticed he was even wearing his hat. She relaxed back on her bed when she saw it was just her uncle.

"Oh. Hi, Uncle Gerry," Kate said.

"Hey, Katie," he said, walking into the room. Kate's mother stayed in the hallway. "Can I sit down?"

Kate didn't say anything but she pulled her knees up to her chest to make room for him on her bed. Gerry sat down beside her on the lavender bedspread.

"Katie," Gerry began, hesitating a little. "I know you said you didn't want to go to the dance tonight. And that's okay, you don't have to. But if you actually do want to go . . . I'd love to take you."

Kate said nothing.

"And if it sucks, we can leave and go get ice cream," he added.

"Gerry! Language!" Kate's mother hissed from the hallway.

Kate thought for a moment, considering the offer.

"But it's a Father-Daughter Dance," Kate said slowly. "And you're my uncle."

"I know," Gerry said, nodding. He looked like he was about to say something else but he didn't.

Kate thought for a moment before she sighed and closed her book.

"I guess that'd be okay," she said finally.

Gerry's face broke into a grin.

"Great! Well, thank you for agreeing to go with me," he said, standing. "I'll be downstairs whenever you're ready."

He left and shut the door behind him. Kate could faintly hear her mother and uncle's voices as they receded down the hallway, although she couldn't quite make out their words as she climbed off her bed. Kate walked to her closet, the door decorated with a cartoon poster she was pretty sure she had outgrown, and opened it. She slowly ran her hands over the dresses that hung in the closet, feeling the soft fabrics slide under her fingers until her hands rested on her favorite green dress. Alone, without any witnesses or expectations, Kate finally allowed herself to smile.

At the dance, Gerry spun Kate on the dance floor for as many songs as she wanted. Her energy seemed boundless and she felt like a leaf, twisting and turning in the wind in her green dress. When they finally took a break and hit the snack table, Kate sipped her fruit punch and surveyed the gymnasium. Whereas the dads at the dance all wore regular suits, Kate's uncle stood out in his dress uniform and she was proud of him. It wasn't the same as being there with her dad, but it was still pretty good. Afterwards, they went for ice cream anyway.

Kate slowly opened her eyes, disoriented by her dream. She momentarily thought that the lights on the ceiling were the lights of the elementary school gymnasium before she remembered that she was no longer 10 and she was in . . . wait, where was she? Kate's eyes came into focus and she glanced around. She tried to think of the last thing she could remember. She went to Central Park for the spaceship landing. Major Anderson brought her into the park. Gerry was there. The aliens came out of the ship. Kate took a picture with her phone and then . . . oh, God. It came back in fragments; the blackout, the gunfire, Major Anderson tackling her to the ground. Then there was an explosion and someone grabbed her arm and then--wait, that wasn't right. Kate closed her eyes, trying to recall. Her eyes flew open and her heart started pounding with adrenaline, her breathing fast and shallow. She was on the spaceship. She was pulled on before the explosion. Kate remembered the alien's three-fingered hand gripping her arm in the ship as the floor moved violently underneath her but nothing after that. Presumably, she'd passed out. At least, she hoped she'd passed out instead of being knocked out. Actually, she wasn't sure which alternative was better or worse, since both of them resulted in her being unconscious on an alien spacecraft.

Kate looked around in a panic, trying to figure out what was happening. She was lying on a metal table and the lights on the ceiling were dim. She looked to her left and saw nothing but blank, white walls. She saw more of the same on the right. She sat up slowly, not even seeing a doorway in the unblemished room. There was only the one table in the center of the room, and nothing more. Just empty space that was almost more frightening than something specific upon which she could fix her fears.

And that's when she realized she was naked.

She looked down at herself wrapped her arms around her torso, drawing her knees up to her chest. Oh god, what had happened? Did they probe her? Was that even a thing? Kate had no frame of reference other than science fiction movies and TV reports from hillbillies, whom she was certain were completely fabricating their stories. Every alien abduction story she'd ever heard usually started with the subject having a "coupla beers" and ended with them waking up naked in a cornfield without their pants. Frankly, that just sounded like a wild Saturday night. Not that Kate ever had wild Saturday nights, not since college anyway. She was in her twenties and felt she should have been experiencing crazy nights, the kind that ended with someone getting arrested and a goat in the back of a cop car. And yet, she spent most of her nights working and researching. Her one real luxury or adventure in life was jogging which felt, when Kate reflected upon it, a little sad. But at least now, she was the only person to have been abducted by aliens in history, which was far more exciting than going for a run. Well, she was the only person if you didn't believe the hillbillies. If you did, then she was just one of many. But at least her abduction was probably caught on camera and wasn't just some tall tale recounted at a bar to anyone who would listen.

Kate barked an awkward laugh at the thought, garishly breaking the silence of the room. She clapped a hand over her mouth, silently swearing. She didn't want them to know she was awake. If she had any hope of surviving these aliens, she needed to be one step ahead of them--unless they were already watching. She looked around the room but saw nothing that would indicate someone could see her, just the empty ocean of white walls. There wasn't even a mirror that could be two-way glass. Although, Kate supposed, if the aliens can master interplanetary travel, they probably had better observational equipment than humans. She let her eyes wander around the room, searching for any kind of clue about the aliens' presence. Could they see her? Were they up on some observational deck, watching to see what she'd do? The thought reminded her of the observational deck of an operating room and she suddenly felt her chest tighten in fear. What if that was the case? What if they were going to dissect her for research? Is that why the alien grabbed her? The table seemed to be the only thing in the room, it would make sense if it were an operating table. Kate suddenly felt like she couldn't breathe. Her breath came in short gasps and panic tingled in her fingers. She closed her eyes for a moment, trying to slow her breathing. She knew panic wouldn't get her anywhere.

In, two, three, four, five. Out, two, three, four, five she counted silently, forcing the air to enter and leave her lungs slowly. The counting reminded her of her jog around New York that morning. Had it really only been that morning? Kate had no idea how long she'd been unconscious. For all she knew it could be next Christmas. She continued counting and the tightness in her chest began to unfurl, slowly, like the petals of a flower. Panicking wasn't going to help the situation. She needed to stay calm. She needed to look at this objectively and not make any rash, emotional moves.

Who, what, where, when, why she silently chanted, trying to focus on the situation like a reporter. It always vaguely reminded her of a board game she'd played as a kid, when she'd have to solve a murder mystery by figuring out who did it, in what room of the house, and with what murder weapon. *Kate, in the spaceship, with the table* she thought to herself. She wasn't quite sure how to use a table that appeared to be solidly connected to the floor as a weapon, but she didn't exactly have any other options in the empty room. If it was all she had, she'd have to be resourceful.

I would definitely lose the board game she thought, snickering rather inappropriately at her predicament. Then again, there was no one around to reprimand her or even glare at her the way Major Anderson had in the park. Major Anderson. Kate wondered what had happened to him. She'd heard the explosion, had he been too close to it? Had Gerry? The suppressed laughter died as tears pricked the corners of her eyes at the thought of her uncle, possibly hurt or killed in the explosion. No, not now. She couldn't think like that right now, not when she had to figure out what was happening. Kate took a deep breath, refocusing her attention.

Okay. Who. She was Kate Porter, daughter of Tom and Miranda Porter, niece of General Gerald Harper. She was a recent graduate of New York University and was currently employed as a fledgling journalist at the New York Eye. At the moment, she was also naked. However, she realized for the first time, she wasn't cold. The air around her skin was exactly the right temperature to keep her comfortable. She didn't know if that was coincidental or something having to do with the atmospheric controls in the ship, but she filed away the observation in the back of her mind all the same.

The other "whos" in question were the aliens. Kate tried to remember everything she could about what she'd seen, recalling the graceful way they'd moved, their humanoid figures, and their facial features. Kate thought of the shorter alien, the one with the blue hair who had stared at her. She couldn't say for sure, but she was fairly certain that that was the one who had grabbed her, not the taller alien with hair like Major Anderson's. She hadn't felt afraid when the blue haired alien had regarded her immediately after disembarking from the spaceship.

In fact, she'd felt almost peaceful when they'd looked at one another. But then he'd grabbed her and dragged her aboard the ship--to save her from the explosion? Or something else, something much more sinister? That was one question Kate couldn't yet answer.

What. Kate had been pulled onto the spaceship by one of the aliens, although for what purpose, she didn't yet know. She knew very little about the "what" other than she was on it in a windowless, doorless white room. With a table.

Where. Again, this was somewhat vague for her. Based on the floor moving under her after she was pulled aboard the craft, Kate figured the ship had taken off again. But because she didn't know how long she'd been unconscious, she didn't know if they'd landed elsewhere or if they were in the sky. Hell, she didn't even know if the ship was in the same galaxy as Earth. She tentatively unfolded her legs and climbed off the table. Her limbs felt stiff but everything seemed to be where it was supposed to be. Glancing around herself to confirm once more that she was, indeed, alone, Kate began to slowly prowl around the perimeter of the room. She walked along each wall, feeling a bit like the narrator in a short story she'd once read. In it, a prisoner is placed in a dark room with a giant pit in the middle of it. There was no pit, but Kate supposed she didn't really know anything about these aliens or this ship. For all she knew, the floor could open up and eject her into space like a used tissue. But if they'd wanted to do that, Kate figured they probably wouldn't have grabbed her and pulled her on board in the first place. Or taken her clothes, because that seemed like overkill. If they were going to eject her into the void, stripping away her clothes seemed a little pointless. However, who's to say that the clothes weren't valuable to them in some way? Maybe cotton (fine, a polyester/cotton blend) was valuable on their planet and they needed her clothes to pay off some sort of debt. But then why bother keeping her? It's not like Kate knew anything about textiles and could help them produce more. At best, she could refer them to some good retail stores in New York but that was about it. She didn't even know how to knit. Her mother had always intended to teach her, but they'd never gotten around to it. Kate sighed. If knitting ended up being the one thing that could keep her alive, she was not going to be pleased.

Kate was hesitant to touch the walls for fear of activating some sort of weird alien alarm that would cause them all to rush in before she could figure out a plan, but she examined them closely, bringing her eyes near the surfaces. All she saw was clean, unbroken space. It looked smooth, like glass. Kate wondered how she'd gotten into the room in the first place with no doors or windows. Maybe the floor? She looked down but saw nothing other than blank floorspace and her own two feet. She walked back to the table and sat down on it again.

When. Kate sat cross legged on the table as she rested her chin on her hand. She felt frustrated by her inability to answer so many of her own questions. The best she could place herself in time was after the explosion, although that really didn't tell her anything. It would help if there were some sort of clock or if she had any idea how long she'd been unconscious, but neither was available to her.

Why. Kate sighed, feeling a little defeated. The only question she could mostly answer was "Who?" and even then, she only gave herself partial credit. Kate had no idea why the aliens had come to Earth in the first place, she had no idea what they were planning, and she had no idea why she was on this goddamn spaceship in this windowless room. She gripped the edge of the table, feeling the metal edge press against her palms and she winced in pain. Kate looked down at her hands and realized the bandage on her hand was gone. The cut was still angry and red across her palm but she figured it would probably heal okay. At least it didn't look infected, so maybe she'd avoided the antibiotic-resistant bacteria after all. Unless the aliens ended up ejecting her into space; apparently, there was no telling what was out there.

Kate heard a noise behind her and she whipped her head around in time to see a door open in the wall on the far side of the room. The panel in the wall slid aside, much like the door to the spaceship had done in Central Park. Kate leaped off the table and tried to hide behind it although, as expected, it offered pretty much no protection. She tried to cover herself with her hands but she felt like her splayed fingers offered about as much coverage as the table.

Kate watched as the shorter alien from Central Park entered the room and the door closed behind it, seeming to reabsorb into the wall. The alien wasn't wearing the spacesuit from the park; instead, its pale skin and humanoid figure was exposed in its entirety although he--she was now certain it was a 'he'--seemed far more comfortable with a lack of clothing than Kate was. *Leave it to me to get picked up by nudist aliens*, Kate thought. She noticed he was carrying some sort of wand in his hand and she felt her chest begin to tighten with anxiety again. The whole being probed by aliens thing wasn't true--or was it? It's not like there's any real frame of reference, Kate was the first abductee in human history, drunk hillbillies notwithstanding. It had to be fake, Kate told herself unconvincingly. It had to be fake. Probing didn't really make sense. But dissection might. Kate's stomach turned threateningly at the new thought. She looked up at the walls again, searching for any sign of a window or air duct. She'd already looked earlier and wasn't surprised to once again see nothing but the blank expanse. Then again, she hadn't found a door when she'd circled the room either and yet the alien had entered through one anyway.

The alien scanned the room and his eyes settled on Kate as the door slid shut behind him. Even in her growing fear, she couldn't help but be struck by the startling clarity of the alien's bright eyes. Looking into them, she almost felt soothed.

Until the alien started walking towards her.

Kate felt her muscles tense into a fight or flight response. She stood up a little, half-crouching behind the silver table. The alien stopped on the opposite side of the table, like they were about to sit down to some sort of interview if there had been chairs present. He set the wand down on the table and Kate took a step backwards, never taking her eyes off the wand. Narrow and silver, it was almost the length of Kate's forearm and had a single green button on one end. Kate wondered what it did and tried not to think of the possibility of it being stuck in one of her orifices.

The alien gestured to her, looking like he was trying to use some kind of sign language as the two aliens had when they landed on Earth. He looked at her expectantly, his eyes wide and questioning. Kate stared at it for a long moment and then quickly shook her head, sure that her heartbeat was loud enough to be heard outside of her body as the blood thrummed in her ears. What was the alien's hearing like? Kate wondered if he could hear her thoughts. If he could, would it even understand them?

Please don't hurt me she thought anyway, just in case. *Please, please, please.*

The alien tried signing again, once more looking at her with hope. Kate crossed her arms over her chest, shaking her head. The alien held out his hand and pointed to his palm. Kate stared at the three-fingered hand, afraid to move. The alien picked up the wand again and started to move around the table towards her, but Kate moved away. The alien rolled his eyes at Kate and for a moment, she wasn't sure if she felt more terrified or annoyed. *For Christ's sake, wh is everyone so condescending today?* she wondered. First Claire, then Major Anderson, now this alien with his weird silver instrument.

The alien moved towards her again and her brain rejected annoyance and locked onto fear. Kate moved around the table, away from the alien, and kept an eye on the wall where the doorway had appeared. She looked straight at the alien for a long moment, locking her gaze on the alien's eyes. They stared at each other. Kate suddenly broke away from the table and sprinted towards the wall. She slammed her hands on the white surface but nothing happened. She felt around desperately, looking for anything, some kind of switch or button, but nothing happened. Kate looked back over her shoulder and saw the alien advancing on her. Kate backed away, not realizing she was backing herself into a literal corner until it was too late. The alien walked closer, wand in hand, and when he was close enough to touch, Kate did the only thing she could think of: she stomped on the alien's instep and punched him in the face. The alien backed up, looking dazed as he gripped its nose, wincing. Kate was suddenly glad Claire had dragged her to that self defense class when they first moved into their apartment.

"You never know what can happen," Claire had said when Kate had been feeling particularly lazy that day and wanted to stay in sweatpants and watch movies instead of going to take a class. "It's important to be prepared for anything."

The wand clattered to the floor. Kate ran for the table and sped to the other side, breathing hard. If she ever got off this ship and back to her normal life, she'd have to thank Claire for making her go to the self defense class. Kate groaned inwardly. Two "thank yous" in a relatively short timespan might make Claire insufferable. But, truth be told, Kate would much prefer dealing with Claire's ego than the alien's probing device.

The alien shook his head before bending down to pick up the wand. He walked back towards the table, a little slower than before and limping slightly. He glared at Kate across the table, although his eyes looked more exasperated than angry. Before Kate realized what was happening, the alien lunged across the table and caught the wrist of her injured hand. Kate shrieked and tried to twist her arm away but for as thin as the alien was, he was much stronger than she'd anticipated.

"No, no, no," Kate repeated, still trying to tug her hand away as the alien pressed the end of the wand against her hand and pushed the green button. The wand glowed and Kate felt panicked tears fall from her eyes as she tried desperately to get away, but the alien held her wrist still. Then the alien pushed the button on the wand again and the light turned off. He released Kate's wrist and she fell back to the ground. She scrambled backwards until her back hit the wall. The alien didn't follow her, but instead watched her with what looked like mild amusement. Kate cautiously raised her left hand to look at her palm and saw . . . nothing. The cut left by the New York City sidewalk was gone. There wasn't even a scar or a mark, nothing to indicate her skin had ever been broken. Kate looked up at the alien in astonishment. The alien pointedly dropped the wand on the table and looked at her, one eyebrow raised. She stood up, feeling a little foolish, and walked slowly back to the table.

"Sorry," she said. The alien shook its head, not seeming to understand. Kate pointed at her nose, then the alien's nose. The alien touched his nose gingerly and nodded, seeming to get what she was trying to say. He brushed off the apology with a nonchalant wave of his hand.

"And thank you," Kate said, pointing to her hand. To his credit, the alien didn't roll his eyes at her again like she'd expected, although this time Kate imagined she deserved it. Instead, he nodded his head graciously. The alien then motioned for her to follow him as he headed towards the wall where the door had been.

"Wait," Kate said. The alien turned at the sound of her voice. "Can I have some . . . um . . ." she said, motioning to her bare body.

The alien shook his head, not comprehending. Kate covered herself as best she could with her hands but the alien just stared blankly at her. She tried pantomiming everything she could think of, from wrapping herself in a towel, to stepping into pants, to putting on a jacket. The alien watched her with confusion before he slowly walked over to one of the other walls and lightly touched the surface with his fingertips. A drawer appeared, springing open into the room. The alien pulled out a folded piece of white fabric and held it out to Kate. She took it and unfolded what looked like a sheet and wrapped it around her like a bath towel. No sooner had she done that when the fabric sucked itself to her body, creating a sort of spandex-type suit that covered her from her torso to her thighs.

"Thanks," Kate said with a smile. The alien continued to look at her like she was crazy but he closed the drawer, shaking his head. Kate was fascinated by the way the drawer disappeared into the wall and wanted to ask more about it, but figured that wouldn't be very productive until she figured out a better way to communicate than acting out a bad game of Charades. The alien motioned for her to follow him again. This time, Kate complied.

Kate, in the spaceship, with the alien she thought as the door appeared in the wall once more at the alien's touch and they left the room.

Chapter 5

The handsome news anchor cleared his throat, somewhat unprepared for the start of the broadcast as he examined the papers on the desk in front of him. He tapped the pages with end of his pen, looking concerned and a bit anxious. He didn't seem to realize the broadcast had started as he reviewed his papers. Suddenly, the anchor's eyes flicked to the camera and he quickly centered himself, turning on his camera-ready self as easily as flipping a light switch when he saw the red eye watching him.

"Good evening. I'm Will Davenport and I'm coming to you live from New York City with breaking news as the situation with the invading extraterrestrials develops. Several blocks surrounding Central Park are still without power and emergency services have been dispatched to the area. After a firefight opened within the park's grounds, there are multiple injuries but, as of yet, no reported casualties. Authorities are advising citizens to return to their homes and stay there until further notice. I'm also getting reports that social media sites like Chatter and Friendspace are currently down because the servers overloaded and crashed. Representatives have said that they are working to fix the issue but, in the meantime, they are requesting that users refrain from trying to access the sites and instead communicate via telephone."

He paused for a moment, cocking his head slightly as he appeared to listen to something the audience couldn't hear.

"And now, we take you to just outside Central Park with Michelle Perry to get some up close and on the ground perspectives on the situation as it unfolds," he announced. "Michelle?"

"Thanks, Will," a pretty, dark haired woman said as the camera cut to her, illuminated only by the light from the camera. "I'm here outside the West 72nd entrance of Central Park where tensions are currently running high as the area is still without power. I've gotten word that some emergency lights are being brought in on generators but, for the most part, this area of the city is still in complete darkness. Sir," Michelle Perry said, stopping a man as he pushed past her in the crowd. "Can you tell us your thoughts on what you saw?"

"I couldn't see much, but it sounded like those aliens set off an explosion and then started shooting at everyone. If that isn't a declaration of war, I don't know what is!" he shouted. "If those space invaders think they can come in here and attack

America, they've got another thing comin'!" He paused for a moment to look down at his cell phone, jabbing the screen with his finger before he let out an exasperated sigh. "Those goddamn aliens are already shutting down our communication satellites! I can't get on any of my social media accounts, they're trying to cut us off from the world!"

"We've gotten reports that the servers are overloaded but the sites should be up soon," Michelle said.

The man looked back up from his phone and stuck his finger in her face, shaking with rage.

"That's what they want you to think! You think this is some kind of coincidence? I'm heading home to get my gun and defend my country *as is my right according to the Second Amendment*," he emphasized, glaring into the camera. The man turned and disappeared into the crowd as Michelle stopped another man.

"Sir, can you tell us what's happening?" Michelle asked.

"My daughter," the man said, his voice cracking. "She was right next to me but I lost her in the crowd when the lights went out. Have you seen her? She's ten years old with brown hair, her name is Beth," he said, begging the camera for an answer. Michelle opened her mouth to speak when the man noticed a policeman push past him.

"Oh, wait, officer! Wait!" the man said, abandoning the camera as he followed the police officer into the darkness. Michelle looked after him for a moment, unsure of what to do, but she finally shook her head and turned back to her task at hand, tapping another young man on the arm.

"Excuse me, can you tell me your thoughts on the incident?" Michelle asked. He was young, maybe fifteen or so, with unruly red hair and angry acne littering his pale skin.

"It was awesome! The aliens knocked out the power and threw down an explosion before skyrocketing back up!" he exclaimed, breathless with excitement.

"You think it's awesome that they detonated a bomb of some kind in Central Park?"

"Well, yeah. I hope they come back and they need volunteers to go with them on their ship. I've met aliens before, you know, so I have experience."

Michelle did her best to refrain from raising an eyebrow at him.

"You have?" she asked skeptically.

"Of course! One night, they visited me in my bedroom."

"And what did they say?"

"Nothing! They didn't say a word, they just took me up on their ship and did experiments on me."

"What sort of experiments?" Michelle asked, trying not to be too obvious as she glanced around for other possible interview subjects.

"They implanted chips in my eyes so they can observe Earth through my eyes without actually having to *be* on the planet."

"Alright, well thank--"

"They weren't the same aliens as these ones. The ones that I met had tentacles."

"Okay, well--"

"And they were orange! Everyone thinks aliens are green, but these ones were bright orange."

"The ones we saw tonight were very pale and definitely not green," Michelle said, unable to resist.

"Well these are *obviously* a different species," the teenager said, rolling his eyes at Michelle's shortsightedness.

"Okay, well good luck with your mission to become an ambassador to the aliens," Michelle said, turning away from him. She heard a warning voice in her earpiece and composed herself, remembering that she was on camera.

"Ma'am," Michelle said, stopping a middle aged woman. She wore loose fabrics and Michelle's nose filled with an unpleasant combination of body odor and patchouli. "Can you tell me your thoughts on what happened here tonight?"

"Oh, it's all just a big misunderstanding!" the woman exclaimed, placing a hand over her heart.

"A misunderstanding? Why do you say that?" Michelle asked.

"Oh, those poor creatures are obviously peaceful!" the woman said. "They had such a lovely glow about them and I just know that they're here to help us!"

"And what about the explosion?" Michelle asked.

"Oh, that," the woman said, dismissing it with a wave of her hand. "We just don't understand their ship technology. There's no need to fear what we don't understand! I'm sure we'll see that these are peaceful, loving beings who want to commune with us and help our sick planet."

"Thank you so much for your time," Michelle said.

"Thank you!" the woman said, grinning broadly before she faded back into the crowd. Michelle stopped another man as he shuffled by. He was elderly, perhaps even in his 80s, with a shock of white hair that looked like he'd long since given up trying to tame it.

"Excuse me, sir, can you tell me your thoughts on what happened here tonight?" Michelle asked.

The old man looked at her and shrugged.

"This is probably it for humanity," the man said.

"You don't think it's possible that they're here on a peaceful mission?"

"What difference does it make to me?" the old man asked. "At best, I've only got a few good years left. Let 'em blow us all up," he said, before turning and shuffling away. Michelle watched him go for a moment before she reached out and tapped a young blonde woman on the arm.

"Excuse me, can you tell me what your thoughts are on the incident, what you saw and heard?"

"My name is Claire Eberhart, I'm a reporter with the New York Eye," Claire said, sounding calm and collected as if she had prepared for this interview. "My best friend and colleague was right next to the spaceship when it landed."

Michelle's eyes lit up.

"You don't say!" Michelle exclaimed.

"It's true," Claire said, taking a breath and glancing down towards her shoes before she continued. "Her uncle is high up in the military so he granted her closer access to the landing to get the story. He would've gotten both of us in," she added quickly, "but I insisted she go alone so as not to crowd the . . . visitors. But now--" Claire paused, appearing to hold back her emotions. "Now, I wish I'd gone with her. Maybe I could have protected her," she said, sounding as if she was trying to keep her voice from breaking.

"Where is she now, have you heard from her?" Michelle asked. Claire shook her head.

"Not yet. But I'm an investigative reporter and I swear I'll use every skill I have to locate her. We've been best friends since college and we work at the New York Eye together. I know her better than anyone. Like everyone else, her phone probably went out during the EMP, but I'm sure once she gets it working again, she'll call me immediately."

Michelle nodded sympathetically.

"Do you think there's a chance that your friend is on the ship?" Michelle asked.

"It's possible," Claire said slowly, seeming to consider the idea. "I'm currently reaching out to my contacts in Washington D.C. to get some more intel on the situation," Claire added, shifting the focus back to herself.

"Do you think you'll really be able to get some information on this incident at this time?" Michelle asked, looking a little skeptical. "I can imagine things might be a little chaotic there at the moment."

"Of course! I obviously can't reveal my sources, but I can promise you that they are very, very powerful people," Claire said. "*Very* powerful. They'll take my call."

Michelle didn't look like she quite believe her, but she didn't contradict Claire either.

"Thank you very much for your time, Ms . . ."

"Claire Eberhart of the New York Eye."

"Right. We'll have more updates as the story progresses," Michelle said into the camera. "Back to you, Will."

"Thanks, Michelle," Will said, the cameras back on him in the safety of the studio.

"Currently, world leaders and their representatives are convening to discuss action against the spaceship," Will continued. "Reports are saying that the ship will be treated as hostile. If the authorities decide to move forward with a retaliatory move, this will be the biggest united military mobilization in recorded human history. There is no word yet on how this will affect citizens across the globe."

"We will continue to relay information as we receive it, so stay tuned for updates as the story develops. Thanks for watching; I'm Will Davenport."

The Washington Convention Center was even more chaotic than the meeting room at the Pentagon had been. The room was enormous and General Harper noticed that several microphones had been set up around the room to, he presumed, make it easier for world leaders to yell at each other like schoolchildren. He had to wonder at the prudence behind this decision to gather as many world leaders as possible into a single space. It seemed to him that if the aliens felt like it, they could just blow up the whole building and send the world into further chaos. Did the aliens even know where they were? Did they know what their Earth's international government structure looked like? Really, the general thought, there was so little they knew about these aliens, particularly in regards to how much they knew about humans. Maybe they knew more than the people on Earth could imagine and they were waiting for an opportunity like this to destroy the international leadership infrastructure in one fell swoop. Or maybe they knew nothing, and that's why they hadn't seemed especially impressed by the vice president. General Harper couldn't blame them if the latter were true--he wasn't a particularly big fan of Harris himself. Less so now that he'd advocated blowing up a spaceship that could contain his niece.

General Harper stood off to the side of the room between Major Anderson and Colonel Hascomb as dignitaries continued to file into the room. Many had already arrived but others were still in transit. However, nobody seemed to be in a patient mood and there was already a passionate fight in progress about the next move in this intergalactic chess game.

"Honestly, I don't understand why this is even a conversation," the British Prime Minister said into a microphone at the front of the conference center. "We clearly need to take military action against the spaceship," he insisted.

"I agree," the German Chancellor said. "They fired upon our planet, we must move quickly."

"It is out of range," the French president argued. "Firing now would only waste our weapon stores and prevent us from taking action when they move back into range."

"How do you know they will come back into range?" the Mexican president asked.

"Of course they will!" the British Prime Minister exclaimed. "What, do you think they're just going to make one stop and then leave us alone forever? Of course not! Don't be daft."

"Prime Minister, I am merely asking a question. I do not appreciate your attitude," the Mexican president said stiffly.

"My *attitude*?" the Prime Minister asked, annoyed. "Extraterrestrials just attacked our planet, what sort of *attitude* would you like me to have?"

"Everyone, please, this is not helping," the Prime Minister of Sweden interjected pleadingly. "We are not accomplishing anything."

As the general watched them bicker, he tried to keep his attention on the discussion at hand but his mind kept drifting back to Central Park. The last he'd seen of Kate, she was standing behind the aliens, her phone raised to take a photo. He'd tried to catch her eye to discourage her, but she hadn't looked in his direction. Knowing his niece, the general knew the avoidance of eye contact had likely been intentional on her part. Kate had always been the ask for forgiveness, not permission type of person ever since she was a kid. She never meant anyone harm, but she didn't always want to wait for some sort of approval process that may or may not turn out in her favor. If she was on the ship, the general hoped Kate hadn't inadvertently offended the aliens or punched one of them in the face.

Unless they were asking for it. Once, when Kate was about seven, she got in trouble at school. Miranda had been unable to leave work in the middle of the day to pick her up so she'd called Gerry to do it.

When he had arrived at Kate's school, he'd found her sitting sullenly in the front office.

"Hey, Katie," he'd said, crouching down beside her.

"Hi, Uncle Gerry," she'd said quietly, not looking at him.

"What's all this about?" Gerry had asked her. "Your mom said you got in a fight? That's not like you."

"It's not my fault," she had said, not looking at him.

Before he'd had a chance to ask her why, the principal had walked into the front office.

"Mr. Porter?" the principal asked.

"General Harper, I'm Kate's uncle," Gerry had replied, standing back up to his full height.

"My mistake, I apologize. I'm Art Henry," the principal had said, extending his hand. Gerry had shaken it, disliking the feel of the man's limp, fish-like handshake. "Come on in, we'll have a chat about what happened today."

The principal had led Gerry and Kate into his office where a playground monitor in an orange vest was waiting in one of the chairs. She stood and introduced herself although the name escaped Gerry now, so many years later. Principal Henry had gestured to the two open chair and Gerry and Kate had sat in them as instructed.

"As you know, there was a little incident on the playground today after lunch," Principal Henry said. He looked at Gerry as if he expected him to say something, but Gerry had said nothing, holding his face passive.

"Kate got in trouble today for fighting," the playground monitor had said.

"What was the fight about?" Gerry had asked Kate.

"She punched a little boy in the face," the playground monitor said. Gerry had ignored her and continued to look at Kate.

"Did you punch a boy in the face?" Gerry had asked her.

Kate had nodded solemnly.

"But it wasn't my fault," she added.

"Young lady, in this school, we take responsibilities for our actions," Principal Henry had said sternly. Gerry had been tempted to shoot him a glare that usually made soldiers sweat but instead he'd continued to focus on his niece.

"Why wasn't it your fault?" Gerry had asked gently.

"He wouldn't stop grabbing the girls," Kate had explained. "We told him to stop but he wouldn't so I punched him."

"Did you tell a teacher?" Gerry had asked.

"I told her," Kate had said, pointing to the playground monitor.

At that point, Gerry had turned to look at the playground monitor.

"And what did you do to stop this boy from grabbing the girls?" Gerry had asked, although he was pretty sure he already knew the answer.

"Well . . . nothing," the playground monitor had admitted. "Kate, when a boy picks on you, that just means he likes you, it's nothing to get upset about, certainly nothing to punch someone over."

Gerry had held up a hand, silencing the playground monitor.

"Let me see if I have this correct," Gerry had said, his face hardening. "Kate and the other girls were being physically assaulted by a boy, even after they told him to stop. Kate brought it to your attention and you did nothing. The boy continued this behavior so Kate took the matter into her own hands and punched him."

"Well . . . yes. But . . ." the playground monitor said, faltering a little.

"General Harper, you know how it is," the principal had interjected. "Boys will be boys. That's no excuse for violence, young lady," Principal Henry said, directing his gaze at Kate.

"Principal Henry, I think you're done addressing my niece," General Harper had said, rising to his feet. "What I'm hearing here--as just confirmed by your playground monitor--is that my niece and her friends didn't feel safe because a boy was assaulting them so they acted in self defense. As a result, Kate is here in the office and the boy is, what, back in class?"

The principal nodded.

"So my niece is harassed, you do nothing about it, and then you punished her, keeping her out of class and compromising her education while that future date raper is sitting in class learning his ABCs?"

"General Harper!" the principal had exclaimed. "Please watch your language!"

"I'll watch my language when you stop victim blaming my niece," Gerry had said. "Kate, we're done here. Let's go."

Gerry had taken Kate's hand in his and left the school. They'd gone back to Miranda's house and made ice cream sundaes in the kitchen. Gerry had even let Kate add more chocolate syrup than he knew her mother would normally allow. He'd thought about a lot of things that day, sitting in the kitchen with his niece, but the one thing he'd said aloud to Kate was that he was proud of Kate for defending herself and her friends.

General Harper glanced over at Ben, who was standing quietly beside him as the heated argument continued to simmer in front of them. The general wanted to say something to comfort him a little, to let him know that he wasn't angry. Except, if the general was being honest, he was angry. At least a little. But he felt more angry at himself for relinquishing Kate's supervision to someone else. All the same, the general still raised his hand and rested it on Ben's shoulder for a moment.

"So what are we going to do?" the Russian president asked. "We are going to prepare for military action, yes?"

"Absolutely," the British Prime Minister agreed.

"And do what, just fire our guns off randomly into the sky?" the French president asked.

"Of course not," the Russian president answered. "We continue tracking the ship and as soon as it is in range, we fire."

"Amen to that," Colonel Hascomb muttered under his breath. General Harper shot him a silencing look and the colonel didn't say anything further.

"North Korea didn't send anyone here, but I know they're on board," the U.S. Secretary of Defense said.

"For once, I actually agree with the little shizer," the German chancellor muttered.

"Oh please, North Korea is going to fire their weapons whether or not we agree," the President of Finland interjected.

"So why not unite together for a common goal?" the British Prime Minister asked.

"Because we don't know what we're dealing with!" the Mexican president shouted, slamming his fist on the table. A chorus of agreement rose up behind him.

"So we should just wait for them to do what they want with us?" the German chancellor asked.

"That is too weak of a position," the Russian president agreed.

"It's not weak to wait for information," the French president insisted.

"Do you want to get your white flag ready now? Why do you even bother having red and blue on your flag when all you use is the white part?" the Russian president jeered, annoyed.

"How dare you?" the French president shouted, jumping to his feet, but he was interrupted by General Harper.

"Everyone, please, this is not helping. Fighting like this only wastes time," Gerry said, taking a few steps forward to mediate the situation. He glanced over at President Wolff who, much like at the meeting in the Pentagon, had yet to say anything. He was watching the argument play out, a slightly amused smile on his face.

"Exactly, we are wasting time. That's why we need to take action now!" the German chancellor exclaimed. Murmurs of agreement could be heard from some of the other dignitaries in the room. The French president gave an exasperated sigh, sitting back heavily in his chair.

"I concur," said the Italian president. "There is no time to waste."

"Excellent, Italy joining up with Germany," the French president muttered, rolling his eyes. The Mexican president snickered.

"Excuse me?" the Italian president asked.

"It's nothing," the French president said, leaning back in his chair with a smug smile.

"It seems to me you have something to say," the Italian president said, rising to his feet.

"Maybe I do," said the French president, standing to square off in front of the Italian president. The two men glared at one another

"Okay, that is enough!" General Harper shouted, his voice booming. Everyone jumped slightly and looked towards him. "Nothing is being accomplished with all of you just snipping at one another like obnoxious children!"

"Obnoxious children? Who do you think you are?" the Italian president demanded, puffing his chest a little as he glared. "On whose authority do you have the gall to speak to me that way?"

"Mine," said President Wolff. The group of dignitaries all shifted their gaze towards him, obviously having forgotten he was even there.

"Keep your dog in check!" the Italian president shouted.

"Dog?" General Harper asked. His anger bubbled inside him and he felt it flood his fingertips.

"Yes! Dog!" the Italian president shouted at him.

"That's enough," Wolff said, quietly and evenly. The Italian president opened his mouth to say more but instead closed it again, shaking his head in irritation and disgust.

"It seems to me," Wolff said, "that we have two courses of action. We can organize militarily and prepare to shoot this thing down the moment it reenters a reasonable range. Or we can wait and see if they attempt to land again and then pursue a purely diplomatic route."

"Those are our only options? All or nothing?" the Chinese president asked.

"You either make a move or risk being taken for a fool," the Russian president said. The Chinese president opened his mouth to speak but Wolff held up his hand, interrupting.

"The question at stake is whether or not we're employing our militaries against the aliens," Wolff said. "Once we decide that, we can decide how and when to proceed. Does that sound reasonable?"

No one said anything, which meant that no one necessarily agreed, but no one disagreed either.

"Alright then, so we're not spending all this time shouting back and forth, why don't we put it to a vote? You can either raise your hand for mobilizing the militaries across the globe or you can raise your hand to exclude military force," Wolff said. "Or you can choose not to vote for either and just live with what everyone decides for you."

The dignitaries grudgingly murmured their assent.

"Okay, let's vote. General Harper, you and Colonel Hascomb count the votes," Wolff said. Gerry and the colonel nodded.

"You too," Gerry whispered to Ben, who nodded as well.

"Alright, all those in favor of using military force, raise your hands," Wolff instructed. The general scanned the crowd, silently counting the hands in his head. Wolff waited until the general and Colonel Hascomb both finished and gave him the go ahead to continue.

"Okay, all those opposed of utilizing the militaries?" Wolff asked. Another set of hands went up in the air and Harper counted again. Once he and Colonel Hascomb finished, Wolff walked over to them and conferred about the numbers.

"Major Anderson?" the general asked.

"I counted the same as you and the colonel, sir," Ben said.

Wolff nodded.

"Alright then. It looks like we have our answer," Wolff said before he turned to walk back to the microphone and make the announcement.

Chapter 6

Kate followed her blue-haired alien out of the white room with the table and into a narrow hallway. She had expected to see flashing lights or control panels like something in a science fiction movie. Instead, the walls were just as smooth and blank as they'd been in her holding room. Kate remembered the way the drawers had seemingly appeared out of nowhere when the alien had touched the walls with its fingertips. She paused, reached out her fingers, and lightly touched one of empty silver surfaces. A drawer opened obediently and Kate stepped back and smiled, pleased with herself. She looked inside and saw a lot of mechanical parts and wires. She didn't know if they were computer parts or cables or what, but the tangle of everything reminded her of the box in her closet stuffed with spare electronic bits and cell phone chargers. Kate wondered if everyone had one of those. It amused her to think that this could be the main point of unity between humans and aliens--an obnoxious mess of computer wires that everyone was too paranoid to throw away in case they'd need them in the future. Even Claire had one, although hers was neatly organized with each wire coiled separately and secured with a twist tie. Kate's collection, on the other hand, was a Gordian knot of complete chaos shoved into the back of her half of the closet. Naturally.

Kate started to lean in closer to get a better look at the contents of the drawer when the alien gently pushed the drawer back into the wall. Kate looked up at him and he held her gaze for a moment, shaking his head, although his eyes didn't look mad.

"Sorry," Kate said, feeling a little sheepish. The alien, of course, said nothing. He turned and motioned for her to continue following him down the hallway. Kate did so obediently, trying to take in as much of the ship as she could see, but the walls were just as empty all the way down the hall. Kate really wanted to keep touching the walls and see what was in the drawers, but she thought that might not make the best impression on her hosts. It seemed like it might be like going to someone's house and rummaging through their dresser or medicine cabinet in front of them. Kate was curious, but not obnoxious. Well, at least not that obnoxious. Not that she ever went through anyone's dresser or medicine cabinet even when they weren't looking. She figured most people had the same type of stuff and she was a reporter, but not much of a snoop. Then again, she'd never been on a spaceship before. However, it occurred to her that she shouldn't drop all of her social etiquette just because she was in space. If anything, she had a greater chance of offending or insulting these aliens and should maybe not keep opening drawers--no matter how badly she might want to.

The alien suddenly stopped and reached out a hand, lightly tapping on the wall with all three of his fingers. A doorway appeared and he stood back, gesturing for Kate to go inside. She walked cautiously to the doorway and looked in the room, unsure of what she'd find. There was a series of monitors on the walls and a shelf full of what looked like maps and files, along with a large window that showed nothing but stars ahead of them. The other alien from the landing in Central Park was also inside, along with a third alien who had curling red hair. Kate took a tentative step forward and the other aliens looked up at her as she entered. They, like her alien, were also disrobed of the suits they'd worn in Central Park and although they appeared comfortable with their own appearances, they seemed surprised to see Kate. The other two aliens looked past her at the blue haired alien and they did not appear to be pleased. Kate glanced back and forth between her alien and the other two and although she couldn't hear anything, they seemed to be involved in a heated discussion of some kind. Kate began to feel uneasy and she edged back a little towards the door. The blue haired alien gently put a reassuring hand on her shoulder and motioned for her to step forward again. She did, hesitantly, and the blue haired alien walked fully into the room behind her. The door automatically closed behind them and Kate felt her muscles begin to tense in a fight or flight response again.

The aliens appeared to continue to silently argue amongst themselves and no one paid much attention to Kate. She glanced around the room, noticing that it looked like a control room of some kind. One wall was comprised of a large control panel but the rest were smooth, save for one shelf next to her that had some texts with a series of symbols on the side that she couldn't read. There was also a small table in the middle of the room and Kate was just glad she wasn't lying on it like an exposed, uncooked turkey. She tilted her head to the side slightly, attempting to examine the symbols on the spine of one of the books. They were completely unintelligible to her, but that didn't stop her from trying to pick out something, anything familiar. Out of the corner of her eye, Kate noticed that all three aliens had turned their attention to her and seemed to be done arguing, or whatever it was they had been doing. She froze, unsure of what to do. The blue haired alien reached past her and pulled out one of the books and set it on the table. He motioned for her to stand at the table so she did, somewhat warily eyeing the other two aliens who still didn't appear to be pleased with her presence. The blue haired alien pointed to Kate and then pointed to the book. Tentatively, she reached over and opened the cover, gently and with care. The book was filled with more of the same unintelligible symbols, over and over again. Kate looked up to her alien who was staring at her expectantly. She shrugged, pointing at the book.

"I don't know what that means," she said, wondering why she kept bothering to say anything out loud when the alien clearly couldn't understand her. Kate glanced over at the other two aliens who looked just as lost as she felt. Her alien pointed again to the book, then to her, and then slowly brought his hands down in front of his body. Kate stared at him, uncomprehending. The alien made the gesture with his hands again and Kate continued to stare, feeling a little stupid for not getting what he was trying to tell her. He made the same motion again, bringing his hands down in front of its body. The gesture kind of reminded Kate of that nursery rhyme "The Itsy Bitsy Spider" when the rain comes down to wash the spider out. She mimicked the gesture and the alien nodded encouragingly. Kate did it again and the alien nodded again, pointing to her. Unsure of what else to do, Kate slowly bent her knees, lowering herself towards the ground. The alien shook his head and did the motion again.

"I don't know what that means," Kate said aloud as she stood up again. "I don't know what 'this' means," she said, mimicking the gesture. The alien pointed to the book. Kate picked it up and the alien nodded, pleased. Kate looked at the pages but they were still covered with markings she didn't know. She looked at the alien who did the gesture again. Kate put the book down. The alien looked defeated, turning hiss gaze up towards the ceiling as if trying to process hiss thoughts or ask God why He'd given the aliens such a dumb Earthling.

"I'm sorry," Kate said. Her alien looked back at her and brushed off her apology with a wave of his hand. He stood for a moment, thinking. Kate looked over at the other two aliens who were watching the blue haired alien, waiting to see what he would do next. Kate didn't know what else to do so she waited along with the other two aliens. Her alien suddenly stood up straight and hurried back to the shelf, pulling out a folder. He brought the folder over to the table and set it down before opening it. Inside were photos and some sort of paper although it looked thicker than the paper she was used to on Earth. Kate reached out a finger and lightly touched the corner of one of the pages and was surprised to feel the coarse texture, almost like linen. The alien began to spread out the contents of the folder. There were photos of stars and planets, some Kate recognized and some she didn't, and there were what looked like star maps printed on the pages. However, Kate couldn't be sure since she barely remembered the astronomy class she'd taken as an elective during her freshman year of college. The alien picked up a photo of Earth and held it up for her.

"Earth," Kate said, unsure of what else to say or do. The alien pointed to Kate and then to the photo. "I am from Earth," Kate said slowly, pointing to herself and then the photo. The alien nodded, seeming pleased. He put down the photo of Earth and shuffled through more of the folder contents until he found the photo of a reddish-yellow planet Kate didn't recognize. The alien pointed to himself and then the other two aliens before pointing to the photo.

"You are from there," Kate said, repeating the alien's gestures towards the extraterrestrials and the photo. The alien nodded, although Kate was pretty positive he still couldn't understand what she was staying. She wondered for the hundredth time why she was still talking if no one there could understand her. She was pretty sure there was some sort of symbolism in continuing to talk when it was pointless and she couldn't be understood, but she was a little too preoccupied with her presence on a spaceship to think about it too deeply. Either that, or she was like one of those Americans who go on vacation to another country and instead of learning the language, they shout in English as if volume had anything to do with the lack of understanding. At least, Kate figured, she hadn't shouted at anyone. Well, as long as no one counted her panic when the blue haired alien had first tried to heal her hand. Kate was pretty sure that punching someone foreign to one's self was probably frowned upon even more than shouting in English.

The blue haired alien pointed to the photo of the reddish yellow planet again before pointing to a location on one of the star maps. Kate leaned closer to look at it although she wasn't quite sure why she did it--she had no idea what she was looking at. She glanced up and saw the alien looking at her expectantly before she shrugged apologetically and straightened up again. Her alien exhaled loudly through his nose, examining all the pages on the table again. He pointed again to the star chart and raised his eyebrows at Kate. She shook her head. The alien looked back to the table, seemingly deep in thought. Kate studied the star charts for lack of something better to do, although they didn't make any more sense to her than they had a minute ago. She was very aware of the other two aliens watching her. Kate wondered if everyone on their planet could read star charts and she just seemed like an idiot to them for having no idea as to how to decipher them. Maybe the aliens traveled around to different planets like this all the time. How many other forms of intelligent life were out there? Thousands? Billions? Kate's head spun a little at the thought of it. Did they all know each other? Was Earth the weird, smelly kid in the lunchroom that no one wanted to talk to or sit with? No, Kate decided. Well, maybe Earth was still the smelly kid in the lunchroom, but there was no way all the other planets were connected. There had to be some out there that were at least more primitive than Earth, right? Kate assured herself that she was probably just being paranoid that all the aliens were hanging out without the Earthlings. *Kate, in the control room, with the conspiracy theories.*

The blue haired alien suddenly straightened up and sifted through the papers until it found another photo. It held the picture up close to Kate and then held the photo of the reddish-yellow planet at a small distance behind it. Kate leaned in close to the new photo and examined it. It seemed familiar and she was sure she'd seen it before. Maybe from her astronomy class, or something at Gerry's house. He'd always liked space and had a huge telescope. Unless work interfered, he was glued to that thing during every meteor shower and every planetary appearance in the sky. Kate thought he would've loved to be in her place just then, for a lot of reasons. She missed him and hoped he was okay, since she had no idea what had happened in Central Park once the ship took off. But if she knew Gerry, he was probably running around putting out fires, both figuratively and literally.

Kate studied the new photo again. It looked kind of like an eye, but not like the God's Eye Nebula. It was longer, like someone had stretched it out, like a . . . like a cat's eye! Of course! Kate's vague memories of her college astronomy class began to come back to her and she recognized the Cat's Eye Nebula. She grinned, proud of herself for recognizing it. She thought briefly that her astronomy teacher would be proud but, in all likelihood, Kate knew her old professor would be somewhat annoyed or possibly offended that Kate had retained almost nothing from her class. The thought occurred to Kate, yet again, that this particular experience might be a little wasted on her. But there wasn't anything she could do about it--they were there, she was here.

The alien emphasized again the photo of the Cat's Eye Nebula with the reddish-yellow planet behind it. Then, it clicked. Kate picked up the photo of Earth and held it further out in front of the picture of the Cat's Eye Nebula. The blue haired alien nodded enthusiastically, thrilled that she seemed to be understanding what he was saying. One of the other aliens, the one with the closely cropped hair like Major Anderson, gently reached over and shifted Kate's hand until it was in proper alignment to the nebula. Major Anderson. Kate wondered if he was okay. She remembered the way he'd tackled her to get her out of the way of the sudden explosion of gunfire in the park. How did that already feel so long ago? It couldn't have been more than a few hours at best, depending on how long she'd been unconscious, but everything in Central Park already felt so far away. Kate supposed that wasn't so off base as her whole planet was literally a great distance from her, but everything felt so disjointed, like maybe she'd dreamed the whole thing.

Kate knew that if Major Anderson had survived whatever happened in the park, then Gerry was probably furious with him. It wasn't Major Anderson's fault though. If anything, he'd probably saved her from getting shot by tackling her the way he had. She wished she had some way of contacting

Gerry. No one had any idea that she was okay, or as okay as she could be while standing naked on a spaceship with aliens with whom she couldn't speak. Although, she considered, maybe they all weren't doing too badly. The aliens had just communicated to her where their planet was and she'd been able to establish trust with the blue haired alien. Granted, the latter had come after she'd punched the alien in the nose, but oh well. There was always a learning curve involved.

What Kate still didn't understand is why she was on the ship in the first place or why the aliens were here. *Where.* Kate had now learned where the aliens were from, even if she still wasn't entirely sure where *she* was in the grand span of the galaxy. All she could see out of the window of the control room was an endless expanse of stars. She thought for a moment, examining the three photographs again. Then she had an idea. Kate pointed the all three aliens and then to the reddish-yellow planet. The alien with short hair like Major Anderson rolled his eyes before he nodded, but Kate ignored him. She then took the photo of the aliens' home planet and made it fly through the air to the photograph of Earth. Kate looked at her blue haired alien and turned her palms up and shrugged her shoulders. The alien stared at her for a long moment, looking as if he was trying to decipher her. Then his eyes brightened as if he understood--or at least had a new idea. He turned to the other two aliens and appeared to tell them something that, of course, Kate couldn't hear. But she supposed she didn't need to because after a brief discussion amongst the aliens, her blue haired friend motioned for her to follow. He led her out of the room, with the other two aliens bringing up the rear, and the party of four walked down the hallway together. Kate noted again the grace with which they seemed to move and she felt a little clunky on her own feet. She tried to step lightly but realized she probably looked like an idiot. Best case scenario, she looked like someone playing Charades and trying to mime skiing. She glanced over her shoulder at the other two aliens and even though they didn't have mouths, Kate was fairly positive they were laughing at her. She returned to her normal gait and accepted her fate as a heavy footed weirdo.

The blue haired alien led the group through a series of hallways and although Kate couldn't be certain, she thought they were heading in towards the center of the ship. The walls were smooth the whole way and Kate had to resist the urge to touch them and explore the hidden storage that she was sure lay behind the unblemished facade. But as their guest, Kate didn't want to be rude. Or was she a hostage? She didn't really feel like a hostage, not anymore, but maybe they were just really nice captors. At least the blue haired alien was. It seemed a little early for Stockholm's Syndrome to be setting in, but Kate had majored in journalism, not psychology, so what did she know? But she was being escorted down a hallway with an alien in front and two behind her so even if she'd wanted to make a run for it, she was blocked on all sides. She didn't think that was the intention of their walking order, but clearly, there was quite a bit she didn't yet understand.

The hallway finally hit an apparent dead end. The blue haired alien turned and appeared to converse with the other two, although this time the conversation was brief. Kate's alien gently, reverently, touched the wall with both hands and a large doorway opened, sliding aside to let them pass. The alien turned and motioned for Kate to follow. She did so without hesitation.

Chapter 7

"We interrupt this broadcast to bring you a breaking news update. I'm Will Davenport with more information on the developing situation with the extraterrestrial invasion."

The news anchor took a deep breath before he continued.

"World leaders are convening in Washington D.C. to discuss a course of action with the extraterrestrials. An announcement has been made that there has been a consensus regarding military action against the aliens is necessary." Will's hands shook a little, almost imperceptibly, on camera. "If this plan comes to fruition, this will be the biggest unified military movement in human history as people around the world come together for a common goal."

He licked his lips, aware that this was the most unsettled he had ever looked during a broadcast, even in his college days. Will had always prided himself on his ability to maintain his cool during stressful situations and here he was, shaking like some nervous jerk on a first date. He supposed that on some level, it was like Earth's first date with aliens. Will considered this for a moment, feeling a little silly for comparing an alien invasion to a romantic rendezvous. Unless, of course, Earth was about to get screwed. The aliens hadn't even bothered to send flowers first.

Will noticed the show producer waving frantically at him from behind the camera. Will then realized he'd lapsed into silence while musing about dates and aliens and he was giving them nothing but dead air. He straightened up in his chair, clearing his throat.

"There is no word yet on how exactly world leaders intend to use this military force, but it seems clear that we as humans are unwilling to give up our home without a fight. There is also no word on the current location of the spaceship. We know it is still nearby, but its exact coordinates are unknown at this time."

Will stopped, seeming to listen to a voice coming in through his earpiece.

"I'm getting reports that the power is now fully back on in New York City, although government officials are still asking for citizens to remain in their homes until more information becomes available. The military is keeping Central Park cordoned off for the foreseeable future and they are asking that citizens avoid the area. We will relay more information as it becomes available, both on the local situation in New York as well as our ongoing coverage in Washington D.C. For the time being, it seems like the citizens of Earth are safe--but we'll keep you posted. And now, back to your regularly scheduled programming. Thanks for watching, I'm Will Davenport."

General Harper snapped off the television, vaguely annoyed by the newscast. The general had noticed the kid's hands shaking while he gave the report, although he doubted most people had noticed the motion. The American people had a right to information, but the general didn't like the undertone of panic in the broadcast. Gerry understood the fear, but he found panic to be a dangerous emotion. Panic is what led people to make rash decisions. Panic got people killed.

Panic, unfortunately, was what General Harper saw before him in the Washington Convention Center. The dignitaries were still arguing amongst themselves, some grumbling about the vote to militarize and others debating about the best way to blow the spaceship out of the sky. Suddenly, the door to his left swung open and two women and a man entered the room, escorted by soldiers. General Harper stepped forward to greet them.

"These are the scientists, sir," one of the uniforms said to the general.

"Welcome," the general said. "I'm General Harper with the United States Army."

"I'm Dr. Annabelle Solomon," the first woman said. "These are my colleagues, Dr. Tom Freeman and Dr. Sarah MacKinnon."

"They're from NASA," one of the military escorts added.

Dr. Solomon raised an eyebrow at him but said nothing.

"Yes, I assumed," General Harper said. "Thank you."

The escort nodded curtly and stepped back.

"Thank you for coming," the general said. "I'm hoping you'll be able to provide some more information on what exactly we're looking at here."

"Yes, well, I'm afraid the information we have isn't much at the moment. Really, you know as much as we do about interacting with extraterrestrials," Dr. Solomon said.

"But you've been following the craft, correct?" the general asked.

"Yes," Dr. Solomon said hesitantly. "But I don't have anything new to report to you. The craft is still in high orbit, out of reach of anything you might want to fire at it. Which, by the way," she added, "I think is a terrible idea."

"I couldn't agree more," the general muttered.

"Sorry?" Dr. Solomon asked.

The general thought for a moment and decided that insubordination was probably the least of his or anyone else's worries right now.

"My niece might be on that ship. As such, I'm hesitant to blow it up," Harper admitted.

Dr. Solomon's eyes widened.

"Really?" she asked, her attention riveted on the general. "Are you sure?"

"I suppose I can't be positive, but yes, I feel fairly certain she is," the general said. "I know a feeling doesn't qualify as conclusive evidence though."

"General Harper," President Wolff said, approaching their small cluster by the wall. "Are these the folks from NASA?"

"Yes, sir," General Harper said. "Drs. Annabelle Solomon, Tom Freeman, and Sarah MacKinnon."

"Mr. President, it's an honor to meet you," Dr. Freeman said.

"Likewise. Now, I need you folks to give some information to the people in this room. We've got some big decisions to make and we need all the intel we can get," the president said.

The scientists all nodded.

"Excellent," the president said, gesturing towards the microphone at the front of the room. The three doctors obediently filed forward to the microphone and the general noted that while Tom and Sarah looked nervous, Annabelle looked cool and calm and just the slightest bit inconvenienced.

"Excuse me, may I have your attention?" Dr. Solomon asked.

The world leaders barely acknowledged her, if at all.

"Excuse me," she said again, a little louder this time.

Still no response.

"HEY!" she shouted into the microphone. For a moment, the room went so silent that General Harper was sure everyone could hear him choke back a snicker.

"Who are you?" the Russian president asked, looking annoyed. The Italian president grumbled an echo to the Russian president's question.

"My name is Dr. Annabelle Solomon, I'm here with my colleagues from NASA to give you all some information about the spaceship."

"Excellent, give us the location so we can blow it up already," the German chancellor said.

The Mexican president rolled his eyes.

"I can give you that information, but it won't do you any good," Dr. Solomon said irritably. "The spaceship is in high orbit, it's out of range of your missiles. But if you'd like to waste your arsenal, be my guest," she added with a smirk.

"What do you know about these aliens?" the Mexican president asked.

"Considering that tonight is the first contact we've ever had with extraterrestrials, not a whole lot," Dr. Solomon admitted. "We are tracking the craft and it seems that although they've retreated somewhat, they appear to be here to stay."

"Here to stay and colonize," Colonel Hascomb muttered.

General Harper had forgotten the colonel was still there and he shot Hascomb a dirty look, silencing him.

"So it is only a matter of time until they get closer and are in range for us to fire on them?" the Italian president asked.

"I would strongly advise against that," Dr. Solomon said.

The Russian president dismissed this statement with a flick of his hand and leaned back in his chair.

"Really," Dr. Solomon continued, ignoring the Russian president. "We don't know anything about them yet and this is our first opportunity to learn from an intelligent life form."

"Until they kill us all," the Italian president countered.

"Think about it," Dr. Solomon said. "When they landed in Central Park, their first instinct was to come out of the ship and attempt to communicate with us."

"Look, Miss Solomon," the vice president started but Annabelle interrupted him.

"Doctor."

"Dr. Solomon. You weren't there, you don't know what happened," the vice president said.

"The whole world knows what happened," Annabelle said. "They got off the ship and tried to communicate with you via some sort of sign language."

"And then they knocked out the power and set off an explosion!" the vice president exclaimed, his voice rising. "Those actions are clearly acts of war."

"What if they're not?" Dr. Solomon countered. "What if they're some sort of misunderstanding?"

A chorus of exasperated groans could be heard throughout the room.

"Why don't you leave the decisions to the big fish?" the Russian president asked condescendingly.

Annabelle narrowed her eyes.

"Because you might be making the wrong decision," she said. "What about innocent lives?"

"Who is innocent, the aliens?" the German chancellor asked.

"Well, yes," Annabelle said, glancing at the general. General Harper shook his head but she continued anyway. "There could be an innocent human on board who would be murdered if you were to blow up the space craft."

General Harper briefly closed his eyes.

"What human?" the French president asked. Annabelle looked at the general and soon everyone's eyes were on him as well. General Harper cleared his throat a little, stalling.

"We have reason to believe my niece could be on board the spaceship," General Harper said. "She was standing beside the ship when the power went out and so far, there are no signs to indicate she was killed in the blast." He thought of the call he'd had to make to his sister. Had it really only been a couple hours ago?

"General," the German chancellor said. "I'm sorry to hear this but unfortunately, sacrifices must be made to ensure the safety of the majority."

"You don't value a human life?" the Mexican president asked, slightly incredulous.

"That's not it at all, I value human life greatly. That's why I think it is important that we act in the best interest to protect as many people as possible," the German chancellor countered.

"Okay, but what about the others?" Annabelle asked.

Everyone's gaze shifted back to her.

"What others?" the British Prime Minister asked. "The aliens? I think we're all comfortable with eliminating them."

"Not all of us," the French president muttered.

"No, I mean what about other aliens?" Annabelle asked. "In all likelihood, this ship is just a scout."

"So then we prepare our artillery for these other hypothetical ships," the Russian president said, rolling his eyes. "Anything else?"

"An attitude of 'well then we'll just blow it up' is nothing but hubris," Annabelle said, visibly angry now. "These extraterrestrials are capable of interplanetary travel. Clearly, their technology is far more advanced than ours. We didn't even know that they *existed* until we saw their ship in our atmosphere. But they knew about us. They knew enough about us to prepare to not only travel to our planet, but land here. What makes you think they won't have more advanced weaponry? Our nuclear weapons could look like sticks and rocks to them. And you're willing to piss them off for some sort of intergalactic dick measuring contest you're sure to lose?"

The general heard Ben snicker next to him and Harper did his best to suppress a smile of his own. He glanced over at President Wolff who wore a bemused smiled on his face.

"Now listen here!" the Italian president shouted, standing up.

"No, you listen!" Annabelle retorted, her voice booming through the speakers in the hall. "You're so eager to blow everything up that you're unable to even consider other possibilities!"

"We have already voted on a course of action," the Russian president said coolly.

"From what I understand, you voted to militarize, not necessarily to fire," Annabelle said.

"To say one and then the other would be redundant," the Russian president said.

"This could be our one chance to broker some sort of peace treaty with them," Annabelle argued. "If we blow up the spaceship, that chance is is irreparably gone. Do you really want to potentially doom our entire planet to annihilation because you're trying to prove a point?"

"How do we even know they're coming back?" the French president asked.

"If my niece is on the ship, they're coming back," General Harper said, surprising himself with his interjection.

"You do not know for sure that she is on the ship!" the Italian president exclaimed.

"And you don't know that they want to kill us all," Annabelle said.

"If the ship comes back into lower orbit, we're opening fire," the British Prime Minister said. "That is all there is to it.

President Wolff looked back to General Harper.

"What do you think?" the president asked. The general sighed.

"I think," General Harper said, "that if they wanted to fire on us, they would have already."

"They already did!" the vice president shouted, losing his cool.

President Wolff didn't take his eyes away from the general, calmly waiting for the rest of his response.

"Like Dr. Solomon said, they have the technological advantage. They've already proven that with their ships and the way they knocked out the power in New York. If they wanted to attack us, they could have done so weeks ago. I really think they want to talk."

"We have already decided on a course of action!" the British Prime Minister insisted.

"I'm not saying we go in blindly and unarmed," General Harper said. "But maybe we wait to see what they want when they land."

"'If' they land," the Russian president said.

"When," Annabelle interjected.

"You're just worried about your niece who was stupid enough to get abducted," the Italian president said, annoyed as he sat down heavily in his seat. General Harper quickly crossed the room and set his hands on the table in front of the Italian president, towering over him. The Italian president's bravado faltered slightly in the shadow of the general but he hardened his face. "And what do you think you're doing?" the Italian president asked.

"My niece," the general said calmly and evenly, "is far too rational and intelligent to think that violence is the only answer. She is currently the closest thing our planet has to an ambassador. I'd advise you against insulting her, as she could be the very link that binds us to the aliens and keeps positive relations as even a remote possibility."

"Or she's been dissected and studied," the Russian president said with a smirk. "The front line usually ends up as cannon fodder, eh, General?"

General Harper stood up straight, doing his best to maintain his composure, although he wanted nothing more in that moment than to lunge across the table and choke the Russian president with his bare hands. It wouldn't be the first time he'd had to do that, although this time he wasn't in a jungle in hand to hand combat. Instead, Gerry was in a room of frightened politicians who just wanted to get the boogeyman before it got them. He stared down the Russian president but the president didn't flinch. The two men stayed locked in an angry glare.

"I think we've all made our points," President Wolff said. "Thank you, Dr. Solomon, for the input from you and your colleagues," he continued, rising to his feet. "I think it would be in our best interest to do as my distant predecessor advised in regards to foreign policy: 'speak softly and carry a big stick.' Although, I can't imagine he expected foreign policy to be quite so foreign as to include aliens."

"Meaning?" the Italian president asked, looking annoyed.

"Meaning," President Wolff said, "that we should prepare our militaries but no one is to fire yet. There's no sense in blowing up a possible intergalactic ally. We don't know what else could be out there"

"We have already decided on a course of action," the Russian president said.

"We decided to militarize. I am not taking away from that," President Wolff said patiently. It wasn't overt, but General Harper thought Wolff sounded a little like he was explaining it to a five-year-old. "I'm just saying we hold our fire until they land. Give them another chance to communicate."

"They already had a chance," the vice president grumbled. Wolff ignored him.

Gerry wondered why Wolff had chosen Harris as a running mate in the first place. At the time, many people thought Wolff should have chosen a warm, engaging running mate like that senator from Vermont or the governor of Oregon, somebody who was popular with people. It's not that Martin Harris was unpopular, but his public image was somewhat bland, like a cracker without the salt. Although maybe that was why Wolff had picked him. Wolff was mysterious. No one could ever really tell what was behind that cool, even facade and dazzling smile. Maybe he picked Harris because Harris was more palatable to the American public, he could temper the unpredictable qualities that made Wolff both intriguing and a little unnerving. If the president was the Wolff in sheep's clothing, Harris was the oblivious sheep who stood beside him. And yet, Gerry considered, maybe there was more going on in that sheep's head than met the eye.

"Let's put it to a vote," President Wolff said, nodding towards General Harper to keep a tally again. "All those in favor of firing as soon as possible?"

The hands were counted.

"All those in favor of waiting until they land and giving them an opportunity to explain?" President Wolff asked.

The other hands were counted, including the doctors from NASA, although Gerry wasn't sure if they were supposed to be in on the vote. He counted them anyway, knowing that those three hands could make the difference between Kate's life or death.

After the votes were tallied and reported to the president., General Harper glanced over at Dr. Solomon. She was watching him, but her expression was unreadable.

"That settles it then," President Wolff said. "Meeting adjourned."

Chapter 8

Kate entered the small vestibule with the three aliens. It was a narrow room, but not uncomfortably so. The blue haired alien appeared to be conversing with the other two, so Kate waited patiently, unsure of what else to do. The room was like all the others: smooth walls, no indication of anything behind them. These walls were white, like the room in which Kate had awoken. The blue haired alien focused his attention on Kate and pointed to the white bodysuit she wore.

"What?" Kate asked, glancing down at herself. The alien pointed again and then waved towards himself. "You want me to take this off?" she asked, pointing to the suit and then she mimed handing it over to the alien, who nodded. "No, absolutely not," she said, shaking her head vehemently. The alien looked exasperated and pointed again to the body suit. "No!" she exclaimed, glancing nervously at the other two aliens, who looked bored. The blue haired alien reached out for Kate's arm and she reflexively pulled it away, nearly backing into the wall. The alien put his hands up in a show of surrender before turning one palm up and pointing to it. Kate looked down at her own hand, the one that the alien had healed. This time, when the alien reached for Kate's hand, she didn't pull away. It took her hand and pointed to her palm.

Who, Kate thought. *The alien who helped me, not hurt me.* When the alien pointed to Kate's body suit again, she gently tugged at the top. It instantly reverted from clothing back to a plain white sheet and weighed heavily in her hand. She handed the sheet to her alien and attempted to cover herself as best she could with her hands. The alien accepted the sheet and lightly touched a spot on the wall. A drawer slid out, seeming to contain what reminded Kate of a kitchen trash can. The alien dropped the sheet inside and the drawer slid back into the wall. Kate felt awkward as she stood naked and exposed in the narrow room with three aliens, her arms crossed over her chest, but she tried to remind herself that she'd been naked when she had awoken on the ship--her exposed body was probably old news at this point. Indeed, the other two aliens weren't even looking at her. Instead, they watched as the blue haired alien tapped another area of the wall and a door slid open, revealing a closet of robes the color of a dark red rose. The blue haired alien passed out robes to each of the other aliens before extending one to Kate as well. She wrapped herself in it gratefully and marveled at how soft it was. It reminded her of one of her mother's hats, a winter cap lined with rabbit fur. Kate had loved that hat when she was little, loved to feel the downy lining. She had been somewhat traumatized at the age of five when she realized it was made from a real bunny rabbit, but she'd become more accustomed to the idea in adulthood. However, she didn't own a hat like that herself, she still couldn't justify the use of a rabbit's fur for fashion. Although, Kate sometimes pondered, she had no problem with leather which seemed a little hypocritical but, short of becoming a vegan, Kate couldn't really do much about that. She'd toyed with the idea of a vegan diet in college, but would usually remember she wasn't supposed to eat animal products around the time she was halfway finished with her scrambled eggs or a pastrami sandwich in the dining hall.

Once everyone was suitably robed, the blue haired alien closed the cabinet door and edged past Kate towards the other wall. The alien pushed his palms flat against the wall and a door slowly slid to the side. The other two aliens filed through the door and the blue haired alien gestured to Kate, as if to say, "After you." Kate held the robe a little tighter around herself and followed the aliens through the door, with her alien bringing up the rear of the line.

The procession led into a slightly larger room than the last, but not by much. There were two metal basins in the center of the room on low pedestals. Kate's alien guided her by the elbow to one of the basins while the other two aliens stood by the other one. When Kate and the alien stood across from one another, the basin between them slowly filled with water from an unseen source. Kate watched, fascinated, as she tried to figure out where the water-- if it was water--was coming from. The blue haired alien tapped her on the wrist to get her attention and she looked up at his face.

"Sorry," she whispered, even the low volume of her voice sounding profane in the silent room. The blue haired alien pointed towards the other basin and Kate turned her gaze in that direction. She watched as one of the aliens, the one with shorter hair like Major Anderson, held out his hands over the bowl, palms up. The redheaded alien scooped up the water with his hands and poured it over the alien's upturned palms, where it ran down in a wash of rivulets until it returned to the bowl. The two aliens then switched roles and the short haired alien poured water over the redhead's hands. Kate glanced back at the blue haired alien who motioned for her to hold her hands out. She did as she had watched the other alien do and her blue haired friend gently scooped water up and let it fall over her palms. Kate was surprised to feel how the water was precisely the same temperature as her skin, so soft it almost felt like nothing falling over her hands. It was definitely a far cry from the hard water in the apartment she shared with Claire and Kim. Kate wasn't sure how she'd be able to go back to using their terrible shower after experiencing water like this, even for a moment as brief as this one.

Her alien held out his hands so Kate did as he had, scooping up the water and pouring it over his three-fingered hands. The alien nodded approvingly. Kate glanced around for a towel but realized that the water on her hands was evaporating at an astonishingly fast rate. She mentally shrugged and waited for further directions. The alien with the red curly hair crossed to the far side of the room and touched the wall. A panel slid aside to allow them entry and all four of them filed through the doorway. They walked into a large room and the first thing that drew Kate's attention was the large, metal, T-shaped apparatus suspended in the center of the room. She looked for strings or a stand of some kind, but found none. The other two aliens broke away and walked off together towards a bench on the other side of the room, leaving Kate alone with the blue haired alien. He gestured for Kate to follow and led her to another bench. They sat together and Kate waited, but nothing happened.

"What are we doing?" she asked quietly, wondering for the hundredth time why she kept asking questions when the alien couldn't understand her. He shook his head and motioned for her to be quiet. Kate didn't ask anymore questions. Instead, she surveyed the room around her. *Where.* Aside from the weird structure in the middle, the room was fairly empty aside from benches placed around the perimeter of the room. There was a table of some kind, not unlike the one Kate had found herself on when she had awakened, but it was raised up on a platform. It reminded Kate of an altar or shrine of some kind, although the table was currently empty. Kate wondered if it wasn't a table at all, but a bed. Maybe all of the aliens slept on metal tables and that's why they had put her on one. From the walk they'd taken to get from the control room to here, Kate surmised they were likely towards the heart of the ship. She wasn't sure if that had any significance yet, but if this was, in fact, a shrine of some kind, then she supposed that made sense.

Suddenly, Kate heard a mechanical whir, although she couldn't be sure of where it was coming from. None of the aliens looked concerned as Kate looked around, but she found nothing indicating a source of the noise. A vibration began in the room, flowing through the floor, the benches, and it even felt like it was physically around Kate in the air. Although she still wanted to find out where it was coming from, she began to relax. The vibration felt like it centered in her chest, slowly sloughing off the mild anxiety she still felt. The longer it continued, the more at peace Kate began to feel. She couldn't remember the last time she'd felt this relaxed. The closest she could think of was when Claire had purchased a massage gift certificate for Kate for her birthday a couple years ago. The gift certificate had been to a place called The

Hushed Lotus, which Kate thought was kind of silly, although she didn't share that with Claire.

When Kate went to the spa, she discovered that no one, not even the receptionist, spoke above a whisper so as to maintain the relaxed atmosphere of the facility. The reception area had been entirely white and lit only by candles, which Kate didn't find to be very practical. But she figured she was only being picky because she was paranoid she'd spill something in the all-white room.

"Welcome to the Hushed Lotus, how may I help you?" the receptionist had whispered.

"I have a massage appointment," Kate had whispered back, feeling a little like she was telling the receptionist a dirty secret. She wondered how the receptionist took any appointments over the phone if she never raised her voice. Kate had wanted to ask, but wasn't sure non-essential conversation was permitted and she didn't want to get kicked out before she had a chance to get her massage.

The receptionist had taken Kate's name and escorted her back into the spa. The white hallways were also lit by candles, and Kate wondered if the spa had skipped out on their electricity bill and were just trying to pretend the whole candle thing was ambiance rather than a necessity. Once they arrived in a small room complete with a massage table and more candles, the receptionist invited Kate to strip down to her preferred level of comfort and informed her that the masseuse would be in shortly.

Once the receptionist left, Kate had a mini-crisis. She had no idea how far to strip down. Claire had told her that she could take off all of her clothes, she'd be covered by the sheet so she wouldn't be exposed, but the idea of lying naked in front of a stranger, even under a sheet, completely freaked Kate out. Her "preferred level of comfort" included sweatpants and a large blanket wrapped around her while she watched bad TV and ate junk food, but she assumed that wasn't exactly what the Hushed Lotus was referring to. As she debated about how much to take off, Kate became even more terrified of the idea that the masseuse might walk in while she was in the middle of taking off her clothes, a possibility she hadn't even wanted to consider. Kate had quickly taken off her clothes, leaving only her underwear, and piled everything on the floor by her purse before quickly climbing under the sheet.

Kate had lain on her back, unsure if that was the right thing to do. She knew she'd eventually have to lie face down on the table, but she had no idea if she was supposed to start like that or not. She had waited under the sheet, feeling awkward as the minutes ticked by. Kate wasn't sure how much time passed, there hadn't been a clock in the room and the candles were lousy for telling time. Just as she was wondering if she should get up and put her clothes back on to find someone, there was a light tap on the door.

"Hello," a tall blonde woman whispered as she quietly opened the door. "My name is Martha and I'll be your masseuse today."

Kate had had a perverse urge to shout, "HELLO, MARTHA!" at the top of her lungs to break up the increasingly unsettling quiet of the spa, but she had managed to restrain herself. Martha motioned for Kate to roll over so she could begin massaging Kate's back. Kate had twisted under the sheet, feeling a little like a fish flopping on a boat deck, but she finally lay on her stomach and got her face in the opening of the table. Due to her anxiety about being so undressed, Kate had expected to feel a little uncomfortable with the whole massage process. But as Martha began gently kneading the stress out of each muscle, working each section of Kate's body like a puzzle, Kate began to relax. So deeply, in fact, that she'd had to catch herself from drifting off to sleep on the massage table.

Kate closed her eyes in the spaceship's sanctuary and leaned her head back against the wall behind her, hoping she wouldn't accidentally activate a drawer that would spring out and smack her in the back of the head.

"Relaxing, isn't it?"

Kate's eyes snapped open and she saw the blue haired alien staring at her.

"Was that . . . was that you?" she asked.

The alien nodded.

"Yes, it's me," the voice said again, although Kate couldn't figure out where it was coming from since the alien didn't have a mouth. At least, not one that she could discern.

"Where is your . . . why can I suddenly hear you?" she asked, revising her question mid-sentence when she realized that her initial question about the location of the alien's mouth might be perceived as rude.

"Communication only works if you are calm," the alien said. "I tried to tell you to calm down earlier," the alien said as he repeated the gesture he had made in the control room, putting out his hands and then lowering them in front of his body. "But I do not think I was very clear."

"No, I think I missed that memo," Kate said with a small, self-deprecating laugh. Of course he'd been telling her to calm down, not crouch down on the floor. Duh.

"Memo?" the alien asked.

"It's just an expression," Kate said, feeling a little silly and her cheeks grew warm. "I just meant that I didn't understand."

The alien nodded and they sat together in silence for a moment.

"So what's your name?" Kate asked. The alien appeared to consider this question for a moment.

"I am not sure how to really explain it to you. I do not think you would be able to pronounce it in its original form, but you may call me Nheri."

"It's nice to officially meet you, Nheri. I'm Kate," she said. Nheri put his hands together in front of his body and bowed slightly.

"It is nice to meet you as well, Kate," Nheri said. "I am sure you have many questions."

"You have no idea," Kate said, her journalistic tendencies clicking into gear. Dozens of questions ran through her mind and the least important one popped out of her mouth first.

"Why was I naked when I woke up?" she asked.

"We only wear suits to protect us from hostile, outside environments," Nheri said, gesturing to himself and the other aliens. "You were so afraid when I brought you on to the ship that I thought removing your clothing would make you more comfortable, make you feel more at home."

"Well, on Earth, we wear clothes all the time. At least, we do in New York," Kate said.

"My apologies, I did not mean to make you uncomfortable," Nheri apologized.

"It's okay," Kate said, feeling a little less violated than she had when she'd first woken up on the ship, although she was glad to currently be wearing the robe. "Why did I have to take off that . . . sheet . . . bodysuit . . . outfit I had on before I came in here?"

Nheri wrinkled his nose.

"It would have been inappropriate," Nheri said. "I understand that you prefer to wear clothes, but that was a rag we use to clean the ship. It was all that was available in that room when you requested clothing. It would be disrespectful to wear it in here."

"A rag? But . . . it changed into clothing when I wrapped myself in it."

"It is the nature of the fabric," Nheri said with a shrug.

Kate thought about this for a moment, wanting to ask more about the fabric, but she thought she might not understand the mechanics of how space fabric worked. That would be a conversation for a later time. If there was a later time.

"So . . ." Kate said slowly. "I have to ask. You didn't . . . probe me or experiment on me or anything like that, did you?"

Nheri's eyebrows furrowed.

"*Probe* you?" Nheri asked, sounding disgusted. "Why would we do that?"

"I don't know. Maybe to study me or something."

"I can study you just fine from over here," Nheri said, shaking his head.

"I'm sorry," Kate said. "I'm not trying to offend you. I'm . . . well, I don't really have much experience with beings from other planets. Any, really. All my information comes from movies and television shows."

"And in these films we *probe* humans?" Nheri asked. "Earthlings are so odd," he said, shaking its head. "No offense."

"None taken, it's an accurate assessment," Kate said, shrugging her shoulders. They sat together quietly for a few more moments. Kate looked over at Nheri, whose brow was still furrowed as he contemplated the ridiculousness of humans.

"Why are you here? I mean, why did you come to Earth?" Kate asked finally.

"Certainly not to probe you. We came to help," Nheri said simply, not offering any further explanation.

"So you came in peace?" she asked tentatively.

"Of course."

"So then what happened in Central Park?" she asked. "If you came in peace, why did you blow out the power?"

"That was an unfortunate coincidence," Nheri said, looking mildly distressed.

"What was that thing you had in your hand?" Kate asked.

"You mean the mechanism with the button?" Nheri asked. Kate nodded. "That was a locking device. We were planned to stay a while to try to communicate with your leaders, so I pushed a button to initiate a locking sequence for the ship."

"You were just locking the ship?" Kate asked, incredulous. She was in disbelief that what was essentially a space car beeper had knocked out the power in multiple city blocks.

"Yes," Nheri said. "Evidently, the device was too powerful for your city's electrical grid." Nehri looked concerned. "I hope we didn't do any lasting damage."

"I'm less worried about a power outage than I am about the explosion," Kate said.

"Explosion?" Nheri asked, confused. "Oh, you mean the engines."

"The engines on this ship explode? That's a little concerning."

Nheri gave Kate a wry look.

"They do not explode, thank you. The propulsion system on this ship is very powerful, it has to be in order to move the vessel, especially on Earth due to the constraints of your gravity," Nehri explained. "Weapons were being fired, we were just trying to get out of there as quickly as possible without injury or damage to the ship."

Kate thought for a long while, processing this new information. The other two aliens appeared to be in a discussion on the other side of the room, their heads bent together. Although Kate couldn't hear exactly what they were saying, she could hear the murmur of a faraway private conversation.

"Why did you bring me on board?" she asked.

"We need your help," Nheri said.

"My help? I'm not sure what help I can offer. I work at a small newspaper on the brink of bankruptcy, I don't think I have any useful skills for space travel. I barely passed my science classes in high school. Hell, I'm not even that good at math, my roommate is the one in charge of our utility bills. I took one astronomy class in college and I remember almost nothing from it!" Kate exclaimed. "I'm sorry, but I think you picked the wrong human. Unless you want me to write a snappy editorial about the ship or your predilection for nudity because in that case, I'm your girl."

Nheri raised an eyebrow at her.

"Sorry, that sounded a little ruder than I intended," Kate said quietly.

"I am not offended. And no, we do not require a 'snappy editorial' about our ship or nudity. But we do need help finding a place, somewhere on Earth."

"Did I mention I'm not really great with geography either?" Kate asked apologetically. If she was the sole representative of Earth, Kate was sure she wasn't doing a great job at trying to prove their status as intelligent life forms.

"You will know the place we seek, I am sure of it," Nheri said, dismissing her protest with a wave of his hand. "Now that we can communicate, I will take you back to the control room shortly so we can discuss it further."

"Will we be able to communicate outside of this room?" Kate asked. "Is the whole ship vibrating?"

"No, but it is not necessary for us to be in here for us to communicate. All you must do is remain calm."

Remain calm while I'm the lone human on a spaceship with aliens who need a navigator, she thought. But instead, she simply said, "Got it."

"One more thing," Kate said. "Why me? Was it just because I was the closest to the ship when all hell broke loose?"

Nheri looked at her curiously, as if the answer should have been obvious.

"You were close to the ship, yes, but that's not why I chose you. I saw you when we disembarked the ship," Nheri said. "You saw me too. I felt a connection with you, I thought you sensed the same thing."

"I did," Kate admitted, remembering the peacefulness she'd felt when she had first met Nheri's gaze in the park.

"Berro was unhappy that I chose you," Nheri said, gesturing to the alien with the short haircut. "He wanted me to get the man in the suit, the one who tried to talk to us, or the one in the uniform with the medals."

Gerry.

"The one in the uniform is my uncle," Kate said.

Nheri studied her for a moment.

"You are close," it said. A statement, not a question.

"Yes."

Nheri nodded, quiet for a moment as he turned his attention to the structure in the center of the room.

"He probably would've been the better choice. He's a general, so he's really great with geography, and he's really into space stuff," Kate said. "Sorry, that last part came out wrong. I meant to say he's really interested in astronomy, so he might actually be able to read your star maps."

"It's alright," Nheri said, his eyes looking amused. "I understood your intent."

"So where is it you're trying to go?" Kate asked. Nheri stood and motioned for her to do the same.

"Come, I will show you," Nheri said. He waved Berro and the red headed alien over and the four of them filed out of the room the way they had entered. When they reached the outermost room, Nheri reopened the cabinet and collected everyone's robes from them and Kate was sorry to return hers. Afterwards, Nheri opened the door to the hallway and gestured to Kate.

"After you," Nheri said.

"Um . . ." Kate said, feeling a little uncomfortable.

"Yes?" Nheri asked.

"Can I have something to wear?" she asked. Nheri tapped himself on the forehead, suddenly remembering, and looked at her kindly.

"Of course."

Chapter 9

"Good evening, I'm Will Davenport with an update on the developing situation with the extraterrestrials," Will said, facing the camera. "We've been getting reports that scientists have met with various world leaders and although we do not currently have access to exactly what was said, we can confirm that the global militarization is still in effect to defend against a potential invasion. As of now, the vessel remains in high orbit around the Earth and the aliens are moving, although we do not know where they are going. The ship does not, however, show any signs of leaving our airspace. As we wait for more information to come in, we take you now to a discussion on humanity's next move with Carl Strauss."

"Thanks, Will," Carl said. He was a larger man, not quite as young or fit or polished as his opening act. He sat behind a desk, which hid the paunch of his stomach rising over his belt buckle like bread dough. He once played football in college but decades later, the taut muscles had softened into a pillowy flab. Beside Carl sat another man and two women. "I'm Carl Strauss and tonight, I have a variety of guests who are weighing in on the discussion of what's going on with these aliens," Carl said. "Tonight, I have Senator Rick Williams from South Carolina, political commentator, best selling author, and frequent guest of the show, Hannah Lupton, and Claire Eberhart of the New York Eye." Carl checked his notes in front of him for a moment as he cleared his throat. The clearing sounded thick and phlegmy, indicative of a two pack a day cigarette habit. "Now Claire, I understand that you have an interesting role in all of this."

"Yes, I do," Claire said, straightening up a little in her chair. "My best friend and roommate has been abducted and is currently on board the spaceship."

"How is that even possible?" Hannah interjected.

"She was next to the ship when it landed in Central Park," Claire explained.

"How do you know she's on board the ship?" the senator asked. "How do you know she wasn't just killed in the explosion?"

Claire rolled her eyes at him.

"Please, everyone who was there at the park knows that she was taken aboard the ship," she said condescendingly.

"So, Claire, what is your whole take on this situation?" Carl asked.

"Well, I think it's pretty obvious," Claire said. "The aliens have taken a hostage and should be treated as hostile."

"Don't you think that's jumping the gun a bit?" Senator Williams asked. "We don't know the exact circumstances yet."

"For all we know, your friend--what's her name?" Hannah asked.

"Kate."

"Kate could have willingly gone on board or even stowed away without the aliens' knowledge or permission," Hannah added.

"Neither of you have even met Kate or know anything about her. I, however, have known her for years, and believe me when I say she's not exactly the adventurous type. There's no doubt in my mind that she's been taken against her will aboard that ship. When was the last time you accused a prisoner of war of this kind of nonsense?" Claire asked.

Hannah rolled her eyes.

"A prisoner of war? Really?" Hannah asked.

"Yes, really," Claire said, narrowing her own eyes.

"A prisoner of war is a strong term," Carl said.

"I'm aware, and I'm not using it lightly," Claire insisted. "The aliens have taken a hostage and detonated an explosive in the park, knocking out several blocks of power and communication. In what universe does that sound like the beginning of a peaceful relationship? When you have dinner at someone's house for the first time, do you steal their dog, shut off their power, and blow up their lawn gnome? Of course not. I don't think this can be viewed as anything other than an opening act of war."

"She has a point," the senator said.

Hannah stared at him.

"Really? Because just a minute ago, you said that she was jumping the gun by saying the aliens should be treated as hostile," Hannah said.

"Yes, but she makes a compelling argument. Peaceful relations aren't begun with destruction and explosives."

"I can't believe what I'm hearing," Hannah said. "You think it's a good idea to retaliate by blowing up something you don't understand without getting all the facts?"

"I never said we shouldn't get all the facts," Senator Williams countered.

"You changed your stance based on the irrational rantings of a girl whose friend disappeared!" Hannah said, hiking a thumb towards Claire. "When was the last time that a rash decision made in anger ever turned out well?"

"I hardly think I'm being irrational," Claire said evenly. "And you're telling me that if one of your friends or family members was forcibly taken, you wouldn't view that as hostile?"

"I'd like to continue this particular topic, but I'm going to have to interject and change gears here a bit," Carl said. "Now, Hannah, I know you've been a longtime commentator on President Wolff, even before he came into office as the president. As someone who has followed his career for some time now, what insights can you offer into what might be going through his mind at this time?"

Hannah took a breath, forcibly looking away from Claire.

"You know, it's hard to say," Hannah said. "Even after all this time, President Wolff's inner thoughts still seem to be somewhat of an enigma. In this day and age of total transparency on social media, it's difficult to say where his head might be at. Of course, this sort of event is unprecedented, so it's hard to anticipate how anyone might react and anything I could say is purely speculation. However," Hannah continued, pausing for a moment, thinking. "The one thing I do know is that President Wolff is careful. Not in a hesitant sort of way, but in a calculated way. It's difficult to know what's going on in his head because his exterior is always cool, calm, and collected."

"Ah, yes, the Wolff in sheep's clothing," the senator mused.

"I'm not saying he's necessarily bad," Hannah said.

"But you're not saying he's good, either," Senator Williams countered.

"Not everyone who disagrees with your political views is bad, Senator," Hannah said.

"Are you insinuating that he cares more about his public persona than he does the welfare of the country?" Claire asked.

Hannah's glare was sharp.

"Of course not. But in this sort of global situation, I think he's going to weigh all of the opinions before making a decision," Hannah said.

"But he's already made one in this unprecedented move of united global militarization," Carl said.

"Yes, but he hasn't fired any shots," Hannah pointed out.

"Not yet, it's only a matter of time," Claire interjected.

Carl nodded, considering this.

"He might not have to be the first one," Carl said, glancing down at his notes. "North Korea has made statements to the press about their intentions to fire nuclear weapons upon the ship if it comes into range above their country."

"Of course they have," the senator said. "Let's be real here, their behavior is a joke. They're constantly threatening to blow everyone up and they have yet to do so."

"Do you really want to poke the sleeping bear and find out what happens?" Carl asked.

"Bear? More like an ornery puppy," Senator Williams said. "North Korea barks, but never bites, and when they do try something, they end up doing little more than embarrassing themselves."

"Well, I have a question I'd like to pose to the whole panel, although I suspect I might be able to guess at some of the responses," Carl said. "What do you think the next course of action should be? What would you propose?"

"I think we should avoid making any rash decisions," Hannah said. "It's likely that they'll land again and then we can have another opportunity to open up a discourse and at least attempt a peaceful interaction."

"And give them the chance to blow up another area of the Earth? What if it's the White House next, or Britain's Parliament?" Claire asked.

"Ms. Eberhart, is it?" Hannah asked. Claire nodded curtly. "Ms. Eberhart, the last time I checked, Central Park was still there. You're concerns about the destruction of the White House seem to be more rooted in science fiction movies than in reality, and I hardly think the aliens share an ideology with Guy Fawkes."

"And how do you know this? Are you in communication with the aliens?" Claire asked snarkily.

"Is that a real question?" Hannah asked, raising an eyebrow.

"Yes, of course it's a real question. Because if your answer is no, then I don't understand why you can assume the aliens are peaceful when there is absolutely no evidence to support that position, especially when they have repeatedly demonstrated hostility," Claire said.

"Well then, what do you suggest?" Hannah asked. "Would you just blow them out of the sky?"

"If necessary, yes. Our home has been attacked and it is our duty to defend ourselves against enemies both foreign and domestic," Claire said.

Both Hannah and Carl gaped at her.

"You'd be in favor of attacking the ship, even at the expense of your friend?" Carl asked.

"Supposedly your best friend?" Hannah added.

"I think efforts should be made to recover any prisoners of war, but sometimes sacrifices must be made to ensure the safety of the majority. The needs of the many outweighing the needs of the few and what have you. I think it's essential to protect our home by whatever means necessary, and a strong militaristic offense is the best way to do that," Claire said.

"How Machiavellian of you," Hannah said, rolling her eyes.

"At least I'm proposing a real solution instead of waiting for the aliens to further attack us," Claire retorted.

"Well, thank God you have no real power," Hannah said as she leaned back in her chair.

"*Excuse me*?" Claire demanded.

"I agree with Ms. Eberhart," the senator interjected. "I think the defense and safety of the majority is of the utmost importance."

Claire smiled smugly.

"What a well thought out opinion that you've just developed over the last five minutes," Hannah said. She muttered something under her breath and while no one could be completely sure of what she said, it sounded vaguely like "spineless idiot."

"That's all the time we have for today," Carl said. "I'd like to thank my panel for being here today, Senator Rick Williams, Hannah Lupton, and Claire Eberhart. I'm Carl Strauss and we'll see you next time. Thanks for tuning in."

General Harper clicked off the television, his annoyance blossoming into aggravation.

"I never liked you," he muttered at the screen where Claire's image had once been as Ben entered the room.

"What was that, sir?" Major Anderson asked.

"Nothing, sorry. Are they ready?"

Ben nodded.

"The president is running a few minutes behind, but everyone else is assembling in the briefing room."

General Harper stood up and followed Ben to the elevator that took them down into the depths of the Pentagon again, back into the secure briefing room they'd met in before. Dr. Solomon was already there along with her colleagues, Drs. Freeman and

MacKinnon, as was Colonel Hascomb. The colonel slightly pulled out the chair beside him and Gerry sat down. Ben stood against one of the far walls.

"Dr. Solomon, nice to see you again," Gerry said.

"General Harper," she said.

Gerry waited for a moment, feeling a little awkward, but then Dr. Solomon turned back to her colleagues and they resumed their conversation in low voices.

"Hell of a night," Colonel Hascomb said with a sigh.

The general nodded.

"Hell of a night," Gerry agreed.

The Secretary of Defense soon entered with the Secretary of State, followed closely by Vice President Harris and President Wolff.

"Well, everyone, let's cut past the niceties and small talk. Where are we with the situation right now? I'm told we have some new intel," Wolff said as he sat down, looking at Dr. Solomon.

"Yes, Mr. President," she said before clearing her throat. "The ship is moving again, still in high orbit. As per your request, we've been able to scan the craft and have located its energy source, should the need arise to blow up our only chance at communication or peace with extraterrestrial life."

"We can do without the added commentary, Doctor," The vice president said, looking more than a little peeved.

"We also have what could be an interesting new development," Dr. MacKinnon said, sitting up a little in her chair. "We've received some scrambled transmissions and although we can't make heads or tails of them yet, it seems to be an obvious attempt at communication from the ship."

"Is there any progress at deciphering it?" the Secretary of State asked.

Dr. Freeman shook his head, his unruly black curls fluttering.

"Not yet, but we're working on it. At present, it seems like our technology is just too archaic for the transmission. It's like we're trying to play the latest video game with top of the line graphics on a 1970s pinball machine."

The president nodded.

"Sounds like a good thing we've decided to stand down and not fire immediately," Wolff said.

"The Earth as a whole is still initiating military mobilization," the vice president said darkly. "This temporary cease fire is just a formality."

President Wolff raised an eyebrow at him but said nothing.

"And we don't know if this is a peaceful transmission they're trying to send," Harris continued. "For all we know, it could a formal declaration of war. There's no reason we should automatically assume it's an olive branch."

"You don't want to give anyone the benefit of the doubt?" Annabelle asked.

A flush spread over the vice president's face.

"Not if all signs have thus far indicated hostility," Harris said, trying to contain his annoyance with Dr. Solomon and failing heartily.

"Not *all* signs have thus far indicated hostility," Annabelle countered.

"Well, I hope something happens soon, one way or the other," Colonel Hascomb interrupted. "People are getting anxious just waiting for the second shoe to drop, know what I mean? I watched this news panel and most of 'em are all fired up to . . . well, fire up at the ship. Did anyone else see that?"

General Harper nodded.

"Wish I hadn't," the general said.

"Hey, do you know that one girl on there? The one who said she's friends with your niece?" Colonel Hascomb asked.

General Harper opened his mouth to answer but Dr. Solomon interjected before he could reply.

"For your sake, I hope not. She's annoying," Annabelle said.

Gerry did his best to suppress a smile.

"So what, is the government just supposed to do the bidding of one annoying blonde on TV?" the Secretary of State asked sarcastically. "If so, we'd have a long to do list from all those reality TV stars."

"Of course not. I'm just saying, there's a lot of unrest. Shouldn't there be some sort of statement made from us? Something that might help people calm down a little?" Colonel Hascomb asked.

"We've issued all the statements we care to make at this time," President Wolff said, sounding a little bored.

"The news program mentioned North Korea," Colonel Hascomb added.

"Oh for Christ's sake," the Secretary of Defense said, pinching the bridge of his nose with one hand. "We've only been dealing with this alien aftermath for a matter of hours and I'm already sick of North Korea."

"Aren't you one of the people who agrees with firing upon the ship?" General Harper asked.

"Yes, but the internationally agreed upon plan at the moment is to hold our fire for the time being," the Secretary of Defense explained slowly.

General Harper narrowed his eyes a little.

"They," the Secretary of Defense continued, "are behaving like an insolent child who wants to kick everyone's sandcastle just to prove they're important."

"I'm not sure there's anything else productive happening here at the moment," President Wolff said, rising to his feet. The rest of the room followed his example. "I think we're at a wait-and-see moment, so there's not much else I can ask everyone to do other than keep tracking the ship and working on that transmission," he said, directing his orders to the three scientists, "and everyone else, get some rest if you can."

The president left then and everyone else slowly filtered out behind him and dispersed in the hallway. General Harper looked around for Dr. Solomon but she was already walking away with her colleagues, engaged in an intense discussion.

"Wake me in an hour, Major," Colonel Hascomb said, clapping Ben on the back, who coughed.

"Yes, sir," Ben said. General Harper stood with Ben for a moment as they watched Colonel Hasocmb walk away.

"Ben, go get some rest," General Harper said.

"But, sir--" Ben tried to protest but Gerry cut him off.

"That's an order. I'll take care of Sleeping Beauty," Gerry said, nodding towards Colonel Hascomb.

"Yes, sir," Ben said, allowing himself to give Gerry a small, grateful smile before he left in search of a couch to crash on. General Harper left the hallway as well, winding his way through the building until he found a break room. He fired up the coffee maker and added hot water. He searched the cupboards and grimaced at the coffee he finally found in the back of the freezer, slightly covered in frost. He added the questionable coffee to the maker and started the machine. Gerry sat down in one of the folding chairs at the small table and wondered why the U.S. Government couldn't swing it to create a slightly less depressing break room. He watched as the coffee started to filter into the glass pot, the dark liquid slowly starting to rise as he waited and listened to the monotonous tick, tick, tick of the clock on the wall.

Tick, tick, tick.

Chapter 10

After Nheri gave Kate a new robe to wear, this one an emerald green, the group of four returned to the control room. The wall of panels blinked slowly, casually, and Kate looked out the window at the mass of stars outside the ship. She glanced back towards the table in the center of the room and saw that the photos and papers were still strewn across the table as they had left them before going to the shrine room.

"So what exactly do you need me to help you find?" Kate asked as she sifted through the photos. She paused, admiring the intricate beauty of the photo of the Cat's Eye Nebula. "Everything here seems way more advanced than anything I've ever seen on Earth, I can't imagine I'd be of much use."

"Ordinarily that would be true," Berro said. Nheri shot him a warning look. "But we need your assistance in a way other than navigation."

All three aliens looked at her expectantly. Kate shifted under their gaze slightly uncomfortable.

"Again, I'm not sure what help I could be," Kate said finally.

"Maybe it will help if we tell you a little more about what we're doing," Nheri said. "We've traveled a great distance to get here, us and the others."

"Others?" Kate asked. "How many others?"

"Oh, hundreds," Nheri said. "Not on this craft though. This is just a scouting ship, the only ones on board are myself, Berro, and Vidda," Nheri explained, pointing to each alien in turn. "And you, of course."

"Where's the other ship?" Kate asked, looking out the window.

"Still on its way, but it should be here shortly," Berro replied. "At least in time for when we touch down on Earth again."

"What exactly are you scouting?" Kate asked. "Earth?"

"Sort of," Nheri said. "Our research shows that your planet hasn't had any contact with other planets, is that correct?"

"Yeah, unless you believe the crazy people who insist they were abducted and probed," Kate said.

"Again with the probing," Nheri said, shaking his head in disgust. "What is wrong with Earthlings?"

Kate shrugged.

"We're a bunch of weirdos," she said.

Berro and Vidda both looked confused and appalled.

"Probing?" Vidda asked finally, speaking up for the first time.

"It's not important, I'll explain later," Nheri said.

"I'd rather you didn't," Vidda said.

Berro still looked disgusted but didn't add to the current topic of conversation.

"Anyway, our research showed that Earth hadn't had any interplanetary contact before. As such, our group decided to send a smaller, scouting ship to initiate contact before we all just showed up at once," Nheri said.

"So you're scouts?" Kate asked.

"Volunteers," Nheri said. "I'm actually in charge of ship maintenance, Berro does security, and Vidda captains the ship."

"What's your function on Earth?" Vidda asked.

"I'm a reporter for a newspaper," Kate said. Vidda looked at her blankly. "I see what goes on and report what I see, and then that information is given to citizens through a newspaper."

"An information officer," Vidda said, nodding as if he finally understood.

"I'm not exactly an officer," Kate said. Vidda looked at her strangely. "I mean, I share information, but not quite like . . . yes, I'm an information officer," Kate said, realizing she was unnecessarily explaining something no one cared about. She also wasn't very interested in delving deeper into her own story when she still had so many questions of her own for the aliens. "So you're a scouting ship for a larger group and you came to Earth to initiate contact."

"That's correct," Nheri said, nodding its head. "But then everything went wrong in New York and it was all a big misunderstanding."

"Right," Kate said. "So then you grabbed me and brought me on board to help you. What do you need me to do?"

"Now that you understand how to communicate with us, we need you to convey that information to the others," Vidda said. "Although you are not the one we intended to bring aboard, it seems we have been blessed and found ourselves with an information officer."

"Okay, I can do that. Or I can try, anyway," Kate said. "Taking off with an explosion like that might have caused some . . . less than favorable views towards you on Earth."

"How do you know?" Berro asked.

"Just a hunch, especially based on the way everyone opened fire in the park," Kate said. "Humans aren't known for being very understanding after a bombing, especially in New York."

"But it wasn't a bombing," Nheri protested. "We didn't mean to cause any damage, it was an accident. We intend to repair the damages and fix anything we might have broken."

"I know that, but they don't," Kate said.

"Well, all the more reason we need you," Vidda said.

"Why are you here?" Kate asked.

"We're here because it's the right thing to do," Nheri said. "We've come a long way but it's for the benefit of your planet. We're here to help, to teach."

"Help with what?" Kate asked.

"Everything," Berro said. "Your planet knows so little."

"Technology and medicine, mostly," Nheri said. "The methods you're using are so primitive, there's so much we can teach you that will greatly benefit your species."

"It's what we tried to tell the men in the park, but no one could understand us," said Berro.

Kate nodded.

"So you're just here to help and then, what, you're going to head home? Stay?" Kate asked.

The aliens looked at each other.

"There is no going back," Nheri said. "Not for us."

"Why?" Kate asked. "If your ship can get you here, can't it get you home?"

Nheri shook his head.

"That's not how it works exactly. You see, our ship doesn't exactly have an engine."

"How is that possible? The boosters from your engine left a crater in Central Park," Kate said.

"The boosters from our propulsion system left a crater in Central Park," Nehri corrected. "In order to travel as far as we did, we had to use a large, stationary launch pad on our home planet that gave us enough power to reach Earth.

"Like a slingshot?" Kate asked.

"Like a what?" Berro asked.

"Nothing, I'm sorry. Please continue," she said.

"The ship has a minor propulsion system, we can go up and down, side to side, but we can't leave to go back to our planet. For better or worse, this is where we live now," Nheri explained.

Kate thought for a moment, trying to process this new information. *Who*. Aliens, apparently hundreds of them in another, much bigger ship. *What*. Information about advanced methods of technology and medicine and everything else, brought on a one way mission. *Where*. Still on the ship, although evidently there was a destination obvious to everyone but Kate at the moment. *Why*. Also unclear. Sheer goodwill towards strangers seemed a little implausible to Kate but then again, she figured she might just be jaded after years of living in New York City.

"Alright, well, I guess that means we're going to have to land so you can try again," Kate said.

"So *we* can try again," Nheri said, a gentle correction.

"Right, so we can try again," Kate said. "Where do you want to land this time? I don't know if New York will be so welcoming a second time after the disastrous first meeting."

Nheri picked up the same book of symbols he'd shown her earlier and handed it to her.

"I don't understand this language," Kate said apologetically. "This all just looks like unrecognizable symbols to me."

"Try again," Nheri urged. Kate opened the book, expecting it to be more of the same as before. However, as she held it, the symbols began to change. They shifted, squiggling around the page as they broke and reformed, until they finally started to reshape into something more recognizable.

"The text works the same way your hearing does," Nheri explained. "When you are calm, it can translate into a language you recognize."

Kate nodded, fascinated. She wished she had her camera with her or at least someone to whom she could show this. Her mother would've loved it. Miranda used to be a professor at NYU in the literature department. Her classes were popular, particularly her more obscure courses in subjects like Icelandic literature. Most people had read some popular canonical British literature like Shakespeare or one of the Bronte sisters, but few had read the Icelandic sagas. Miranda's classes always filled up quickly and often had extensive waiting lists. Kate's mother actually spoke six or seven languages, Kate had stopped keeping track a long ago. Her mother loved to read books in their original language whenever she could. She always said it enhanced the literature, that so much was lost in translation, but she appreciated those translations because they enabled her to share wonderful books with those who might not otherwise have been exposed to them. Something like this book from the aliens would open up so many doors in literature for her mother's classes.

Former classes. Kate still kept forgetting. Her mother had tenure at NYU, but was currently taking a sabbatical while she tried to fight her cancer. Kate thought that was a pretty awful way to spend a sabbatical. Miranda should've been traveling or writing a book or learning another language. She'd been working on Hungarian when she got her diagnosis but Miranda had put that aside for now, always saying she was too tired. Kate hated watching her mother fade in front of her eyes. Miranda kept trying to paint a rosy picture for Kate, claiming she felt so much better these days, but Kate had a suspicion that her mother was lying. She also suspected that Gerry knew the extent of the severity of her mother's cancer, but neither of them had divulged the information. Kate figured that her mother didn't want her to know how bad it was, so Kate did her best to play along. It was the least she could do.

Or was it? A thought occurred to Kate. Nheri said they had come to help humans, to bring them more advanced technology and medicine. Could they cure cancer? Could they fix her mother? Kate had no idea if something like cancer even existed on their planet. Maybe it had and they'd eradicated it? She didn't want to let herself hope only to set herself up for failure, but maybe, just maybe, her mom could finish learning Hungarian.

Kate wanted to ask about the medical technology they had, but she knew it wasn't the appropriate time. Nheri, Berro, and Vidda were the ones who needed help now; Kate's mom could wait. Kate knew her mother didn't have much time, but if this second landing went well then maybe Miranda wouldn't have to wait for very long.

Kate pulled her thoughts away from her mother and refocused on the book in her hands. She began to read the words on the page as they shifted into focus and was surprised to recognize the text in front of her.

"Are you serious?" she asked, looking up.

All three aliens nodded gravely.

"I assure you, we are very serious," Nheri said. "This is not something we take lightly."

"Of course, I'm sorry, I didn't mean to offend you. I'm just . . . surprised," she said. "I sort of assumed that this was just kind of an Earth thing, not an intergalactic thing."

"It's most certainly not 'just an Earth thing'," Vidda said, sounding a little annoyed. Beside, him Berro bristled a little.

"I'm sorry, I know that now," Kate said quickly. "I really don't mean to offend anyone, I'm just trying to catch up and understand what's going on here."

"It's alright, I know you've never met anyone from another planet before," Nheri interjected, seemingly more for Berro and Vidda's benefit than for Kate's. The other two aliens seemed to relax a little at the reminder of Kate's Earthling ignorance. Kate wanted to add more, but decided not to continue digging herself in a hole and instead, she turned her eyes back to the text. She continued reading until the *Where* and *Why* fully clicked in her mind, a revelation that finally rendered the clarity she'd been chasing since she woke up on the ship.

"Oh my god, that's why you're here?" she asked, pointing to a spot in the text. Nheri leaned over to see where she had placed her finger and nodded.

"Can you help us?" Nheri asked.

"Yes."

Chapter 11

General Harper was staring at his second cup of coffee, exhaustion tugging at the corners of his vision, when Major Anderson lightly knocked on the open door of the break room.

"Sir?" Ben said tentatively.

"What is it, Major?" Gerry asked. He noticed for the first time that the table in the break room where he was sitting was slightly sticky. Why was it sticky? There was nothing in the break room but coffee, not even a few packets of sugar or creamer. The general wondered why he even cared that the table was sticky at all. It's not like he was moving in or anything. He tapped his fingers on the table a few times, feeling his skin cling to the table before releasing with a small "shick shick shick" sound. Was it someone's birthday? Had someone brought in cake or something? Whatever it was that made the table sticky was clear, maybe someone had spilled a clear soda on the table during the birthday celebration. Maybe there was no birthday at all, maybe someone had just knocked over a soda and hadn't bothered to clean it up. Although nothing else appeared to be sticky, at least the floor wasn't. Did someone spill water on some sugar? But there weren't any sugar packets in the drawers. At least, not anymore. Maybe that's what happened to them, the last was ruined and the break room hadn't been restocked. Who was in charge of that sort of thing? How long had this break room been without sugar packets and creamer? Had there ever been sugar packets and creamer in this break room? Maybe this was just known as the break room with the terrible black coffee. Gerry continued to muse over this until he realized Ben had been talking and Gerry hadn't heard a word.

"I'm sorry, my mind was elsewhere," the general said, trying to regain his composure with a shake of his head. "What did you say?"

"I said that we have some new intel on the spaceship. It's moving," Ben repeated.

"Where's it going?" Gerry asked, rising to his feet. He dumped out the remains of his coffee in the sink and tossed the empty styrofoam cup in the trash. He then briefly turned on the sink, letting the water splash away the remaining droplets of the coffee that clung to the stainless steel like ticks on a dog.

"It appears to be heading towards the Middle East," Ben said.

"Aw, Christ. With our luck, they're going to want to land right in the Gaza Strip," Gerry muttered. "Alright, let's start mobilizing everyone."

"Everyone?" Ben asked. "Internationally, too?"

Gerry nodded as he briefly tried to rub some life back into his eyes.

"Yeah. After how delightfully that meeting at the convention center went with everyone, I'd rather not, but I'm not about to start a global incident right now," Gerry said as he gestured for Ben to lead the way out into the hallway.

"About a global incident . . ." Ben began hesitantly as they walked down the hall towards a bank of elevators.

"What?" Gerry asked, dozens of scenarios immediately breaking out in his head. Did Russia already fire on the ship? Did some of the warring countries in the convention center declare war on one another? Which one of them bombed France?

"Well, it seems that as soon as there was intel of the ship moving again, North Korea fired at it."

"They *what*?" the general exclaimed, his voice sonorously filling the bare hallway.

"The bomb didn't really do anything," Ben said. "The ship was--and still is--in high orbit so there's no way it was even going to get close, even if the bomb was made properly. It burst in the air like a cheap firework and what was left of it fell into the ocean."

Gerry gave an exasperated sigh as he pinched the bridge of his nose. He wished he was pinching the head of the North Korean leader instead.

"Like a kid with a freaking toy rocket launcher," he muttered. "Other than North Korea, has anyone else made a move?"

"No, everyone else is in accord with the agreement we reached at the convention center," Ben said. "Some begrudgingly, but they're complying all the same. They're just waiting for our signal."

"Well, get everyone to start heading towards the Middle East--do we know specifically where yet?"

Ben shook his head.

"Okay, mobilize everyone but *no one does anything without a direct order from me.*"

Ben nodded.

"Yes, sir."

Gerry turned and looked down the hallway, suddenly remembering.

"Guess I'd better go wake up the colonel," Gerry said as he started to walk away. He stopped, and looked back to Ben just as the elevator doors opened. "Did you get any sleep?"

Ben shook his head.

"No, sir."

Gerry felt disappointed and silently promised himself he'd find some time for Ben to take a break. Gerry nodded and turned, leaving Ben to get on the elevators as Gerry left in search of the colonel.

The general finally found him splayed out on a couch in an unoccupied office. Colonel Hascomb was a large man and the couch sagged under his weight. The colonel's mouth was open as he slept and loud snores grumbled from his throat like an engine. A shiny line of drool had eeked out of the corner of his mouth and Gerry watched him for a moment. He felt slightly repulsed, although this was by far not the most appalling thing he'd ever seen in his life. One doesn't get to be a four-star general just by staring at photos of roses and puppies. Maybe it was the exhaustion from the long night, but Gerry's nose wrinkled at the large man splayed on the couch. Maybe it was the vulnerability of an otherwise important man, or just the baseness of a human at rest. Whatever it was, Gerry was too tired to think about it at length at that exact moment. He reached out a hand and grasped the colonel's shoulder, shaking him gently. Not gently enough, it would seem, as the colonel started violently, swinging out a fist that would have connected with the general's jaw had Gerry not jumped back.

"What? What's going on?" the colonel asked, disoriented. His eyes slowly focused on General Harper. "Oh, General. I'm sorry," he said, rubbing his eyes as he stood up. "Did I just take a swing at you?"

"Yes, but I don't take it personally," Gerry said. "The ship's moving, we need to go."

Colonel Hascomb pushed himself up, stretching out his back with a loud crack as he did so and the two men left the office.

"Where's it heading?" Colonel Hascomb asked.

"Middle East."

The colonel snorted derisively.

"Of course it is. Couldn't land in a field in Montana, could it?" the colonel asked.

"Apparently not."

The two men reached the bank of elevators and pressed the button. They waited, not speaking. Colonel Hascomb continued to rub his eyes and he gave a loud and wet sniff as he tried to wake himself up. Gerry watched the numbers above the elevator door light up as it drew closer to their floor and wondered if he should've taken a nap instead of drinking that vile coffee. He's not sure which situation would have left him worse off. But what was done was done, time wasn't going to turn back for his convenience.

The elevator dinged politely and allowed the two men aboard.

"Think we have time to hit the food court before we head out?" Colonel Hascomb asked. General Harper didn't acknowledge the question so the colonel turned his gaze to the numbered buttons. The general actually would have liked to stop for some food and kind of wished he'd thought of it earlier instead of just drinking that awful excuse for coffee, but now there was no time. Up on the ground level, the general and Colonel Hascomb were met by Ben who led them out front to a waiting black SUV. The leather still smelled new when General Harper climbed inside and he wondered if it was. It very well could have been, but there could also be a hidden air freshener under the driver's seat. Gerry supposed it didn't really matter and he ultimately didn't care, but the last government SUV he'd ridden in had smelled like stale cigarettes so he was pleasantly surprised at such a nice-smelling car.

The car took them to the airfield where a plane was waiting in the gray early morning light. The general, Colonel Hascomb, and Major Anderson all boarded the plane where they found the Secretary of Defense, the vice president, and the three scientists from NASA.

"May I?" Gerry asked, gesturing to the open seat beside Dr. Solomon.

"Sure," she said, nodding. He sat beside her as a flight attendant closed the door to the plane. They sat quietly together during take off as the engines roared and the pilot pulled them skyward. No one on the plane was really saying much of anything. As soon as the silver bird was in the air, the vice president dozed off, breathing heavily but not snoring. Gerry glanced over at Ben and was relieved to see he had nodded off as well. Finally, the poor kid was getting a break.

"So, we're heading to the Middle East?" Gerry asked.

"Yes," Annabelle said. "Specifically, Israel."

Gerry stared at her for a moment.

"You're kidding."

"I certainly am not," she said, looking a little insulted. "You think I can't read my own data?"

"No, I don't mean . . . when I first heard the ship was coming down in the Middle East, I made a joke about it landing in the Gaza Strip," Gerry explained.

"Oh," Annabelle said, relaxing a little. She even allowed herself a small smile. "Well, according to my calculations, it's not going to land in the Gaza Strip. Near it, but not in it."

"The aliens couldn't have picked a less volatile spot?" Gerry asked with a sigh.

Annabelle shrugged.

"I guess not. Unless . . ." she started but then hesitated.

"Unless what?" Gerry asked.

"Unless they've been studying Earth and have a reason to pick Israel," she said.

"You think they've been studying us?" he asked.

"Why not? It doesn't seem like an accident to me that they chose to land in Central Park. Their technology is obviously far more advanced than ours so it's not only possible, it's probable," Annabelle said.

"I guess that makes sense," Gerry said thoughtfully.

"Of course it does," Annabelle said, the smile fading from her face.

"You don't really take a lot of flack, do you?" Gerry asked.

"No. I can't imagine you do either."

Gerry shook his head.

"No, I don't," he agreed. They were quiet for a moment. "So I know what this is like for me as an army guy, but what's this whole thing like for you? I mean, as a scientist," Gerry asked.

She looked at him for a moment, seemingly trying to gauge his intent, before she answered honestly.

"It's the single most incredible thing to happen in human history," Annabelle said. "Logically, it always made sense that there were other intelligent beings out in the universe, but intergalactic communication has always been a big 'if.' Before this ship appeared, we knew absolutely nothing. But now," she said, her eyes shining as she spoke, her reserved exterior starting to fall away. "Now, we've already seen and learned so much, even through the brief landing that happened in Central Park. This is our first, possibly only chance to really learn something amazing and new and I'd hate to see it squandered away because of a few trigger-happy dignitaries," she said quietly, eyeing the sleeping vice president.

"I can't promise what will happen when the ship comes down, but I'll do my best to keep that from happening," Gerry said.

"I appreciate that," Annabelle said.

Gerry looked around the plane to see that everyone else on board besides them had dozed off. Colonel Hascomb was starting to snore again but softly this time, more like a loud kitten purr.

"Did I hear," Annabelle started, glancing around the plane to be sure everyone else was asleep. "Did I hear that North Korea launched a nuke?"

Gerry hesitated but then nodded.

"Yeah. They launched something, anyway. It blew up in the air, no harm done other than to embarrass themselves and irritate everyone else."

"I see," Annabelle said, thinking for a moment. "What's your niece's name? The one that's on the ship?" Annabelle asked.

"Kate. She's my sister's kid."

"Are you close?"

Gerry nodded.

"I'm sorry, it must be hard having her up there," Annabelle said.

"Thanks. It is, but there's not a whole lot I can do except try to keep someone from blowing up the spaceship before it has a chance to land."

"God, I'm so jealous of her," Annabelle said. Gerry gave her a perplexed look. "Oh, I'm so sorry, I'm not trying to make light of her situation. As her family, I imagine it's terrifying. But as a scientist, I'd give anything to trade places with her to see the inside of the ship."

Gerry nodded.

"I understand. If I know Katie, she's probably trying to explore every corner and she's opening doors and cabinets she's not supposed to. She's a reporter--writes for a newspaper--but even as a kid, she was always asking a hundred questions.

Going anywhere with her was a nightmare because we had to sit and talk about it for twenty minutes beforehand. Why were we going to the grocery store? What were we going to buy? Why did we need to buy it? How far away was the store?" Gerry said as he smiled at the memory.

"What paper does she write for?" Annabelle asked.

"You haven't heard of it," Gerry said.

"Come on, try me. I might surprise you."

"The New York Eye."

Annabelle thought hard for a moment.

"Okay, you're right, I haven't heard of it," Annabelle said. "I admit defeat. Is it a good paper?"

Gerry considered this question before choosing his words carefully.

"Kate's pieces are good," Gerry finally said.

"Not exactly a first-rate paper?"

"It'd be generous to call it third-rate," Gerry said. "But it was one of the only places willing to hire her fresh out of college so she jumped at the chance."

"I would think . . ." Annabelle said, trailing off at first. "I'd think she would've been able to get one of the bigger publications to look at her considering her . . . family connections."

"What connections?" Gerry asked, a little confused. "Her dad passed away when she was little and her mom is a professor at NYU."

"I mean you," Annabelle said. "Not everyone is related to a four-star general. I know that's not exactly getting hired for the right reasons, but let's be honest--sometimes it's all about who you know."

"True," Gerry said. "I can't argue that. But I don't think the thought even occurred to Kate and if it had, I don't think she would've acted on it. She really wants to do things on her own terms, always has. The only thing she's ever asked me for was access to the landing in Central Park, and even then . . . I don't know. I doubt it was her idea."

"Whose was it then?"

"If I had to put money on it, I'd say her friend, Claire. The one who was on that TV panel talking about the aliens."

Annabelle rolled her eyes.

"God, that girl is a piece of work," Annabelle said.

"Don't I know it," Gerry said. "But Kate's been friends with her since college. They're still roommates and they work together at the New York Eye. I don't know what Kate sees in her, but no matter how insufferable Claire is, Kate is always the first to defend her."

"Maybe she sees something the rest of us don't," Annabelle said. "Although if her TV spot is any indicator of her true personality, Kate must have a third eye, or at least the patience of a saint to deal with that girl's bullshit."

Gerry laughed.

"You're probably right," he agreed. Their conversation lulled contently for a moment and Gerry admitted to himself that he was glad everyone else on the plane had dozed off.

"Do you have any kids of your own?" Annabelle asked.

Gerry shook his head.

"Nah, I'm married to the army. Besides, Kate was more than enough for me, you know?"

Annabelle nodded.

"I know."

They sat in silence for a while and Gerry looked out at the window, down at the blue of the Atlantic Ocean far below. He didn't think he was that tired, he felt like he'd gotten his second wind, but he suddenly felt Annabelle shaking him awake. He opened his eyes and winced at the painful crick in his neck.

"Sorry to wake you, but we're landing," she told him.

"Thanks," he said, rubbing his neck. "Didn't realize I'd fallen asleep."

"You fell asleep mid-conversation. Either you were really tired or I'm exceedingly boring company," Annabelle said.

"Definitely not the latter," Gerry said. "I didn't snore, did I?"

"No, but it was difficult to hear anything over Colonel Hascomb's snoring, so it's hard to say for sure," Annabelle said.

Gerry smiled.

After the plane touched down in the airfield, General Harper could see that they weren't the first arrivals to the party. Several other countries' aircrafts were already present and the day was warm, an angry wind blowing about them as they disembarked. They were personally met by the Chief of General Staff of the Israeli army.

"Welcome to Jerusalem," the rav aluf said. "Come, there is no time to waste," he said, pointing towards something in the sky that seemed to grow bigger by the second. It took Gerry a moment to recognize what it was. The spaceship.

"Are we almost there?" Kate asked, peering out of the control room window. Even from this great height, she could see the hordes of people gathered below. She hoped Gerry was one of them.

"Almost, we'll land shortly," Vidda said, coming to stand beside her.

Kate felt a tap on her arm and turned to see Nheri, holding out to her the clothes she'd worn earlier, neatly pressed and folded.

"For you," Nheri said. "I thought you might want your clothes back for when we land."

"Thank you," Kate said, accepting the clothes.

"I can take your robe for you if you wish," Nheri said, holding out his hand.

Kate glanced down at the green robe.

"Could I maybe . . . go somewhere else to change?" she asked. "I'm not really comfortable just stripping down here."

"Sure," Nheri said, although he looked a little confused by this request. Kate figured that was probably justified, considering they'd all seen Kate naked already, but Nheri didn't object. Nheri led Kate out of the control room and back to the room in which she'd originally woken up on the ship. At least, Kate thought it was the same room, although she could have been wrong. There weren't exactly any defining features about this room to mark it as her own. Maybe most of the rooms on the ship were blank white rooms with metal tables in the center.

"Will this do?" Nheri asked.

"Yes, thank you," Kate said. Nheri held out his hand for the robe and Kate obliged this time, holding her folded clothes to her body as best she could to cover herself. Which was silly, she thought, because Nheri had already seen her naked. A lot. Her bare body wasn't anything new to him and, really, it didn't even seem very interesting to him. For all she knew, the aliens found her nude body grotesque and they were all just being polite. However, she was glad for the privacy when Nheri left the room. Kate dressed, but not before once again marveling at the way the ship's air was never cold on her skin. It was a small thing, but she hoped that was one of the technological advances the aliens planned on sharing with Earth. Sure, she'd obviously prefer a cure for cancer or AIDS or world hunger, but having a perfectly temperature controlled apartment didn't sound too bad either.

When she had secured the last button on her shirt and slipped on her shoes, Kate walked over to the wall through which Nheri had exited. She pressed her hands on the wall as Nheri had but nothing happened. She tried moving her hands around, running them over the smooth surface, but the wall remained a wall.

"Um . . . Nheri? Hello?" Kate called. She tried another spot on the wall and a large cabinet swung open, revealing a stack of white cloths similar to the one Nheri had given Kate when she woke up. Kate closed the cabinet and was about to call again when the door slid open, about five feet to the right of where she'd attempted to open it.

"Thanks. I got stuck, I guess," Kate said. Nheri motioned for Kate to follow it back into the hallway.

"Understandable," Nheri said. "I suppose if you're not used to it, you wouldn't know where to put your hands."

"Can you see door and cabinet outlines on the walls? Or do you just know where everything is?" she asked.

"I know where everything is," Nheri replied. "I don't mean to sound arrogant, but I am the ship's maintenance officer. It's my job to know this ship as intimately as my own hand."

"Of course, I should've thought of that," Kate said. They walked silently side by side for a moment. Kate once again became aware of how awkward and clunky her steps seemed compared to Nheri's grace. This time, though, she refrained from altering her gait.

"Are you nervous?" Kate asked as they drew closer to the control room. "About landing again?"

Nheri nodded.

"Nervous, yes. New York didn't go as we had hoped, which, I imagine, sounds like an understatement. But I'm also excited. I have waited for my whole life to come here and it is finally happening," Nheri said as they reached the control room. Kate wanted to ask so many questions about Nheri's age and lifespan, but she didn't know if that was a rude thing to ask like it was on Earth. And really, if things didn't go well when they disembarked, their lifespans could be cut short today. Nheri and Kate walked inside the control room and she looked out the window, noticing that the ground was much closer than it had been before she left. She also noted that both Berro and Vidda now wore the same blue suits they'd worn in Central Park.

"Are we landing?" Kate asked.

"Soon," Nheri said. Kate glanced back over her shoulder to see Nheri wrapping himself in one of the blue suits. When he was done, Kate saw the neatly folded red robes on the table. They looked to be the same as the ones they'd worn in the inner sanctuary of the ship.

"Good," Kate said as she turned to the window. She squinted and could make out the individuals within the crowd that had gathered around their projected landing site. Then she realized the closest people weren't just onlookers--they were soldiers. She felt her heartbeat quicken and she sucked in a breath. *Stay calm*, she told herself. *You have to stay calm. Your life and those of the aliens might be entirely contingent on you staying calm.* It dawned on Kate that it might be a bad idea to put the pressure of saving four lives on herself when she was attempting to stay calm, so she made herself change her train of thought. *Who. The aliens and me. Which sounds like a terrible title of a cheesy kids movie. What. Helping the aliens complete their mission. Where. Jerusalem, like that won't be a total shit show. When. Very, very soon. Why. Because it's the right thing to do.*

"When we land, be sure to let me go first and do the talking," she said. "I don't think anyone down there is going to be calm enough to hear you."

All three aliens nodded before each put on one of the red robes. Kate admired the trio of them for a moment, realizing how elegant they really looked, when another thought occurred to her.

"And for God's sake, do *not* lock the ship this time!"

Chapter 12

When the ship touched the ground, the air around it was tense and hard. The crowd seemed scarcely brave enough to breathe and the weapons of the international armies were trained on the ship. General Harper and the rav aluf stood beside the ship and Gerry felt his heart jackhammering in his chest. He tried to remember a time when he'd been this nervous during a military operation, but he couldn't think of one. In fact, when he thought about his years of service, he often felt a strange detachment. He'd lost friends, brothers in combat, some of whom had died right in front of him. And yet, when he reflected on it now, it was like he was skimming the back cover of someone else's story. He still remembered everything, or at least a lot of it, but nothing seemed quite as significant as this moment, right here. Gerry tried to tell himself that it was because of the aliens and that this moment was unlike any other in human history, save for the disaster in Central Park, but he knew he was lying to himself. This moment was so important to him because he knew he was about to find out if Kate was alive or dead. Gerry had convinced himself she was on the ship, but he knew there was a strong possibility that she wasn't there. Maybe she had died in the park, had been too close to the explosion. No one had found anything yet to indicate a casualty, but they didn't understand the extent of this alien technology. Who knew what the effects of a detonation like that would have on a human being? It blasted a crater in Sheep Meadow, for God's sake. Gerry wasn't much of a praying man, but he silently begged God, the universe, or whomever else might be listening that his niece would be alive, but he braced himself for the alternative. He had already rehearsed the next call he'd have to make to his sister and he wasn't looking forward to it. Miranda had already lost so much and it broke Gerry's heart to have to be the one to tell her that her only child was gone, this time with certainty.

A warm breeze blew over the crowd as the ship stayed silent and motionless. Then, suddenly, a young woman's voice came over a loudspeaker.

"Uncle Gerry? Are you there?"

Although it had been the very thing Gerry had prayed for, he was still stunned to hear his niece's voice.

"Gerry?" the voice asked again. "General Harper?"

Gerry realized he hadn't actually responded yet.

"Katie?" Gerry called, breaking his stoic, military reserve for a moment. "Is that you?" Out of the corner of his eye, Gerry could see the rav aluf watching him. Gerry was sure the rest of the world was doing the same thing.

"I'm coming out," Kate said. "Please don't fire, it's just me coming out right now."

"Hold your fire!" Gerry shouted towards the poised armies.

"Is he too close to the situation for this?" Dr. Sarah MacKinnon whispered to Dr. Solomon. Annabelle shrugged.

"Maybe. Or maybe his close connection is what's keeping those tanks from blowing up the ship immediately," Annabelle whispered back, nodding to the row of tanks pointed at the spaceship.

The panel in the spaceship opened, sliding into itself to reveal a doorway. Kate cautiously took a step out of the ship. She held some sort of small device in her hand, which didn't go unnoticed by the armed forces surrounding her. There was a sound of weapons shifting in their positions around her and she froze.

"I said hold!" the general yelled. Glancing around, he could tell that some of the soldiers weren't pleased with this, but they followed orders all the same. Kate said something into the device in a low, murmuring voice. This sort of thing might have otherwise gone unheard but the unnatural silence in the crowd made her somewhat audible.

"Close it now," Kate said. Her voice was even but Gerry could see that her eyes were scared. She scanned the crowd until she saw her uncle and then she started walking towards him. Kate could feel some of the guns following her but she did everything she could to keep calm and keep breathing normally. The closer she got to her uncle, the faster she walked until he caught her in his arms and hugged her as tightly as he could. The rough fabric of his uniform felt scratchy against her cheek but she was so relieved to see him.

"Katie, my god, I'm so glad you're okay," the general said, not wanting to let her go, but he pulled back and looked her up and down. "Are you okay?"

"Yes, I'm fine," she said. "More than fine, actually," she said, holding up her hand as proof. Her uncle looked at her blankly. "Remember? In the park, I told you I cut my hand. They fixed it for me."

"Who fixed it, the aliens?" Annabelle asked, coming forward cautiously to stand at the general's elbow.

"Katie, this is Dr. Solomon," Gerry said without glancing back at Annabelle.

"Nice to meet you," Kate said. "And yes, they did." Kate briefly looked past them to see Major Anderson standing back with the others. He looked stoic and reserved as always but when she met his eyes, relief broke through his firm expression.

"How?" Annabelle asked, unable to help herself.

"Don't we have other things to talk about right now?" Colonel Hascomb asked, joining the small group. "In case you all forgot, there's a giant spaceship in front of us."

"No, really?" Kate asked with exaggerated sarcasm as she rolled her eyes. "I'd completely forgotten where I just spent the last several hours."

"Katie . . ." the general said warningly. Kate didn't say anything else but she glared at the colonel anyway. She did, however, notice Annabelle cover her mouth with her hand to hide a smile.

"What happened up there? Why are they here?" the general asked, trying to redirect his niece's focus. "They didn't . . . hurt you, did they?"

Kate shook her head.

"No, they're really nice. They fixed my hand, remember?" she asked, holding it up. "And by the way, they're a little appalled at the idea of experimenting on people."

"Well how would I know that?" the general asked.

Kate shrugged.

"You wouldn't. I didn't either. But now they may or may not find science fiction movies horrendously offensive."

"Well, we'll be sure not to invite them to movie night," Colonel Hascomb interjected. "For chrissake, why are they here?"

Kate shot him a dirty look before turning back to her uncle.

"They're here peacefully," she said. She heard the colonel snort derisively but she ignored him. "Really, they are. They're here on a mercy mission to help us. They have so much they can teach us and they want to help unify mankind."

"Why?" Gerry asked.

"They said they feel like it's their duty and responsibility to help us. Their calling, I guess," Kate said.

"Then what was the deal with the blackout and the explosion in Central Park?" Colonel Hascomb asked. "That doesn't exactly seem like they're showin' up to the party with fresh baked muffins."

"That was an accident," Kate said. "When Nheri pushed that button, he was just trying to lock the ship so they could stay a while, they didn't know it would cause a blackout."

"He?" Annabelle asked, intrigued.

"Yeah," Kate said. "They don't like to wear clothing indoors."

"What these aliens do or do not have in their pants still doesn't explain the bomb," Colonel Hascomb said, raising his voice a little.

"Wyatt."

It was only one word from General Harper but it had the desired effect as the colonel didn't say anything further.

"The explosion was also an accident," Kate said.

"Convenient," the colonel muttered.

General Harper shot him a look.

"Everyone started shooting and they had to get out of there or risk damage to the ship or injury to themselves. The launchers on the ship had to give it enough of a boost to get out of range," Kate said icily, glaring at the colonel as she did so.

"Okay, so they're peaceful and they're here to help," Gerry said. "How did you even learn all this? No one could understand anything in the park."

"Is that a translator?" Annabelle asked, pointing to the small black device in Kate's hand.

Kate shook her head.

"No, this is like a walkie talkie. They gave it to me so I could tell them when it's okay to come out."

"So then how do you communicate with them?" Annabelle asked.

"You have to be really, really calm," Kate said. The colonel snorted again. "I'm sorry, Colonel, can I get you a tissue or something?" she asked, annoyed.

"Listen, young lady--" Colonel Hascomb started.

"*Wyatt.*"

Colonel Hascomb fell silent once more and the general looked back to Kate.

"Okay, let's try it. I'll tell everyone to keep standing down, you tell them to come out," Gerry said. He gave the order as Kate spoke quietly into the transmitter, giving the aliens the all clear. Then they all turned back to look at the spaceship.

The door opened again and immediately the air felt so thick with anticipation that Gerry felt like if he stuck out his tongue, he could taste it. An alien emerged, one the general didn't recognize from the park, wearing a red robe. It clashed slightly with its red hair but Gerry thought that complementary colors was probably not high on the priority list at the moment. The alien held a device up to its face, where its mouth should have been, and Kate slipped her hand into her uncle's.

"Remember, stay calm and take slow breaths," Kate whispered. Gerry nodded. He felt Annabelle take his free hand.

"Hello, everyone," Vidda said into the device, which turned out to be a microphone of some kind. "Thank you for allowing us to land on your planet once more. I want to begin by offering our sincerest apologies for the misunderstandings that transpired in New York. Please be assured that we will repair any damage we caused."

"I can't hear a damn thing," Colonel Hascomb muttered.

"Shh!" Annabelle hissed, her attention rapt.

"We are here on a mission," Vidda continued. "You are in desperate need of help. It is why we have journeyed here, because we wish to make your situation better for you."

"Mommy, I hear it!" a little boy in the crowd of civilians behind the soldiers cried, tugging on his mother's hand.

"Don't be silly, there's nothing to hear," his mother said, bending down to pick him up.

"But I hear it!" he insisted.

An old woman standing nearby approached them and touched the boy's hand.

"I hear it too," she said quietly.

The boy's face broke into a smile.

"Told you," the little boy said to his mother, more than a little smugly.

"You really hear it?" the boy's mother asked the old woman.

The woman nodded.

"As clear as a bell," she replied.

"We hope to share and teach and help you grow as a planet," Vidda continued. "We are honored to be guests in your land and hope this will be the beginning of a peaceful time between your people and ours."

A rabbi in the crowd nodded approvingly.

"But before we begin, there is something we must do. We have traveled so far and for so long, and we must complete our pilgrimage. Thank you so much for opening your holy city to us. Please be assured that we will give to it the reverence and respect it deserves."

With that, Vidda put the device in a pocket of the red robe. Nheri and Berro stepped out of the spaceship and joined Vidda on the ground. The door slid shut behind them and Nheri turned to Kate and put up its hands. She nodded, smiling a little.

"What was that?" Gerry whispered to Kate.

"I made them promise not to try to lock the ship again," Kate said.

The world watched as the three aliens all put up the hoods of their red robes and began to walk in a single file line. The crowd parted like the Red Sea, but none of the weapons wavered from their targets.

"Wait, did they say they're here on a pilgrimage?" Annabelle asked, deeply confused.

"Yup," Kate said, nodding.

"Aliens from another planet are here. In Jerusalem. For a pilgrimage," Annabelle said slowly, emphasizing each point.

"It's been a strange day," Kate said.

"They really came for this?" Annabelle asked. "Where are they going?"

"It looks like they are heading towards the Church of the Holy Sepulchre," the rav aluf said, speaking up for the first time.

"The church of the what?" Colonel Hascomb asked.

"The Church of the Holy Sepulchre," the rav aluf repeated. "Where Jesus of Nazareth was crucified and entombed."

"Holy shit," Colonel Hascomb said, understanding finally flooding him.

"Excuse me? Holy what?" the rav aluf asked, looking offended.

"Ignore him, it's just an inappropriate saying," General Harper said quickly, pacifying the rav aluf as he narrowed his eyes at the colonel. The small group lapsed back into silence as they watched the backs of the red robes retreating towards the holy site.

"Are they here to stay?" the general finally asked.

"Yes," Kate replied.

"For how long?" Gerry asked.

Kate sighed.

"Do you remember learning about Hernando Cortez when you were in school? He was an explorer and a conquistador."

"Vaguely," Gerry said slowly.

"When he arrived in Mexico with his men, he burned and sank his ships to remove any chance of retreat," Kate said.

"Are you saying they're going to burn their ship?" Gerry asked.

"I'm saying they already have. In a sense, anyway," Kate said. "Their ship is on a one way trip. They're here for the long haul, however long that ends up being."

"Wasn't Cortez responsible for wiping out the Aztecs?" Annabelle asked.

"Yeah," Kate said. "I don't think that's their intention though."

Thoroughly annoyed with the conversation, Colonel Hascomb walked away, leaving the general and Annabelle with Kate. General Harper considered this information for a moment as he watched the aliens walk away.

"This is weird," he finally said.

Kate glanced up at the sky and saw the larger ship floating above them. Gerry and Annabelle followed her gaze towards the ominous, looming spacecraft.

"I think it's about to get really weird," said Kate.

About the Authors

E.S. Fortune is the evil genius behind 1602 Enterprises. When he's not running an empire or concocting weird and wonderful stories, he enjoys spending time with his three kids in his home state of Texas.

Emily Regan received her M.A. in creative writing from Northern Arizona University and is the author of several books, including the recent *What's an Adult? No One Knows Anything and We're All Going to Die.* She currently resides in northern Arizona with her husband, son, and two dogs who sit patiently at her feet while she writes (the dogs, not the husband and son).

www.ingramcontent.com/pod-product-compliance
Lightning Source LLC
Chambersburg PA
CBHW072104170626
46813CB00004B/1451